W9-AVB-384

Nine-year-old Neil McDonald has always wanted to write a book. Every time he tries, though, it comes out 'like the Hardy Boys or something'. But when a maverick substitute teacher challenges him to record all the events and thoughts of a single day, the doors of creativity swing open. It helps that the day in question is, in Neil's words, 'pretty weird'. The time is the fall of 1971; the setting is 'North America's northernmost metropolis'. The cast includes Neil, his best friend Keith and his gnome-like baba, a budding Black Power advocate, the heavy-smoking son of anti-war activists, and a very small boy wielding a very large axe in a public park. Neil thinks his day will climax with the broadcast of the first night game in World Series history, but what he's in for is something much deeper, a surprise that will teach him much about the world and his place in it. In the end, Neil has his book. And it's nothing at all like the Hardy Boys.

IAN McGILLIS

A Tourist's Guide
to Glengarry

The Porcupine's Quill

NATIONAL LIBRARY OF CANADA CATALOGUING IN PUBLICATION DATA

McGillis, Ian, 1962–
A tourist's guide to Glengarry/Ian McGillis.

ISBN 0-88984-246-9

I. Title.

PS8575.G4435T68 2002   C813'.6   C2002-905160-6
PR9199.4.M28T68 2002

Published by The Porcupine's Quill,
68 Main Street, Erin, Ontario NOB 1TO.
www.sentex.net/~pql

Represented in Canada by the Literary Press Group.
Trade orders are available from University of Toronto Press.

We acknowledge the support of the
Ontario Arts Council, and the Canada
Council for the Arts for our publishing
program. The financial support of the
Government of Canada through the
Book Publishing Industry
Development Program is also
gratefully acknowledged.

ONTARIO ARTS COUNCIL
CONSEIL DES ARTS DE L'ONTARIO

The Canada Council | Le Conseil des Arts
for the Arts | du Canada

For Padma

* * *

This is weird.

That's what I was thinking, standing there in Irene's, on my last night in Glengarry.

Just being in Irene's was weird enough. It's this little place over on 82nd Street. They call it a diner, but you don't really see anybody dining in there, unless you call sucking on cigarettes and guzzling coffee dining. It's a really long, thin room, like a one-lane bowling alley, with tables down one side, and a poster by the door of an upside-down monkey with a long tail saying 'Hang in there, baby!' Being there was weird for me because it was ten whole blocks from my house, it was dark outside, and I was by myself.

Another strange thing was who I saw sitting at the table by the window. It was Mr Baldwin, a substitute teacher who taught my grade four sometimes, and Mr Nedved, one of the janitors at St Paul's, my school. You don't expect to see teachers and janitors hanging out together, especially outside school, but these guys aren't exactly your typical teacher and janitor. They didn't notice me at first, so I walked a few tables past them.

It must have looked pretty funny to see this little kid standing in the middle of a diner at night blinking from all the smoke, because almost everybody stopped smoking and yakking for a second to look up at me. I started to wish I hadn't gone in there, but it would have been chicken to just go out again. The jukebox was playing 'Maggie May', which was the number one song on the CHED countdown the week before. It's this really long song, by a singer with a croaky voice, about a guy who skips school and hangs out in poolhalls. So I was trying to hide how nervous I was by concentrating on the song when I heard a loud voice from behind me.

– Hail, hail, the wandering bard!

It was Mr Baldwin. He was talking to me. I walked over.

– Welcome to our bohemian enclave, he said. A cup of absinthe?

Just like in school, I didn't really know what Mr Baldwin was

7

talking about. Half the time he'll talk to you just like he'd talk to an adult, and it's up to you to figure out what he's saying. I don't mind that, though. It's kind of neat. He just assumes you're smart. He pulled a chair over and nodded at me to sit down.

– So, what brings our pocket Tolstoy into this disreputable den? he asked.

Tolstoy's this writer guy from Russia. Mr Baldwin calls me that because a few weeks before, at the start of the school year, I told him I was thinking about writing a book. It's one of those things you say and feel stupid about a minute later, but he took me seriously, and ever since then he's talked to me like I was a real writer.

– I was just walking around, I said.

That wasn't the whole truth, but you couldn't call it a lie, either.

– Gathering material, no doubt, Mr Baldwin said. All grist for the mill, eh?

– Yeah. I guess.

I had no idea what he meant. Then he turned to Mr Nedved.

– I should tell you, Jacek, that our little friend here is no ordinary gum-chewing, slingshot-shooting tyke. He's about to storm the ramparts of the literary establishment.

Mr Nedved looked like he didn't exactly understand Mr Baldwin, either, probably because he's still learning English. I could tell from the books on their table that that was why they were there, so Mr Nedved could get English lessons. He raised his eyebrows and smiled at me. That was neat, because he's not a real smiley guy. He didn't say anything, though.

The waitress came by and filled their coffee cups, and then Mr Baldwin gave me a serious look. I think it just occurred to him how unusual it was that I was there.

– If you don't mind my saying so, you're looking a tad troubled, he said.

– I'm okay, I said.

Actually, I wasn't so okay, but it was a long story. I'd had a really weird day, and I'd sort of wandered into Irene's without really knowing what I was doing. I didn't want to interrupt the English lesson, though, so I didn't get into it. Then Mr Baldwin stuck his finger in the air.

– Of course! he said. Writer's block! What else could have you looking so flummoxed? The creative juices are dammed. The words just won't come. Am I right?

– Yeah.

The funny thing was, I hadn't even started this book I told him I was going to write. I like the idea of writing a book, but I can never think of stories.

– A word from the wise guy, said Mr Baldwin. There's a little exercise for scribblers in your spot, recommended by no less than Hemingway himself.

Finally, I thought, I knew what he meant by something. Hemingway was this writer who also went fishing a lot. At home there was this old copy of *Life* magazine, with a picture of him smoking a cigar and holding a giant swordfish. He also did this thing they do in Spain where you get a bull mad at you and the bull chases you around trying to gore you. Later, he shot himself.

– What exercise is that? I asked.

I thought he meant stuff like jogging and push-ups.

– It's a kind of plunger, if you will, for those in your predicament, he said. Simply choose a day, any day, and write down everything that happens to you.

– What do you mean, everything? I asked.

– The works.

– Even going to the bathroom and stuff?

– There's no room for squeamishness in your trade, lad. The great writer follows his characters everywhere, even to the meditation room.

There he went again, from talking about the bathroom to some other room that's not even in my house. Mr Nedved seemed confused, too. He kept drinking coffee.

– Should I write about just what I did, or what I thought about, too? I asked.

– My lad, these decisions are in your hands alone. Just tell it like it is. Remember Joyce. No bodily function is too low, nor any interior musing too lofty.

He'd lost me again. Who was this Joyce lady I was supposed to remember? I was starting to like his idea, though. It kind of solved my problem of not being able to make up stories. Whenever I try, it ends up sounding like I'm copying the Hardy

9

Boys, and I don't even like them. Maybe just writing stuff down would be interesting, at least for me. It was a pretty good time to do it, too, because the day I'd just had – October 13th, 1971 – was a pretty weird day, like I already mentioned.

– Okay, I'll try it, I said.

I must have taken a long time to say it, because they were back into their English lesson. Mr Baldwin didn't hear me at first.

– What's that, young sir? he asked.

– I'm gonna try it.

– Excellent! Excellent! I feel honoured, indeed humbled, to have performed this small service to future centuries of readers. Take out thy quill, and may it serve thee well.

– Sure. Thanks.

I wanted to say more, but they were starting their lesson again, Mr Baldwin explaining to Mr Nedved how to order beer in English. So I stood up and tiptoed to the door. 'Maggie May' was still playing, it's so long. Just as I was opening the door, I felt a hand on my shoulder. I turned around and it was Mr Nedved. He smiled at me and said something in Czechoslovakian. Then I left.

So now I'm back at home, sitting in the empty living room. It's about midnight, and Mum and Dad and all my brothers and sisters are in bed. I'm not supposed to be up, because there's a big day ahead of us tomorrow, but I really feel like writing this stuff down before I start forgetting everything. I've got Dad's flashlight to see with. My pen is making a giant shadow on the wall where the painting of the blue heron used to be. It's weird to think I might never see Mr Baldwin and Mr Nedved again, to show them what I've done.

✦

ONE

There's this thing I do every morning, at least every morning since I've been sleeping on the bottom bunk of the bunk-bed, with my brother Duncan on top. (I used to sleep on top until I fell off one night, so Mum made me and Duncan switch. The only trouble is, Duncan's way heavier than me, so his mattress presses down pretty close to my face.) What I do is play a game with the pattern on the bottom of Duncan's mattress. Paisley, Mum told me it's called. I start down in the bottom left corner with my finger, and pretend the finger is a mountain climber or explorer. What I have to do is make him climb from that corner to the top right corner. It sounds easy, but the pattern is really complicated, and I have this rule that if I stop or lose my way, the guy dies, frozen to death or eaten alive by a rare mountain leopard or crushed by an abdominal snowman. So I have to concentrate really hard, even if Duncan's making fun of me or Mum's yelling from downstairs that I'll be late for school or Sam, our dog, is trying to stick his nose in my gaunch. I always tell myself that if the guy makes it, I'll have a good day, and if he doesn't, something bad will happen. Today, he made it. I'm not so sure that means anything any more.

I got up and got dressed in the same clothes I wore the day before. Some people think it's a big deal to change clothes all the time, but I don't see the point. Once me and my friend Keith Puzniak had a contest to see who could go the longest without changing. We got to two weeks, but then people started getting mad at us. They'd walk the other way when they saw us. Anyway, I figured I'd be playing football at recess, so why wear clean clothes just to get them dirty again?

I went downstairs. It's weird, because even though our family is big, with seven kids including me, I hardly ever see anybody except Mum at breakfast. Dad goes to work at some crazy time before the sun's even up, and all my brothers and sisters leave for school before I'm up. I always wait until the last minute. So this morning it was just me and Mum again.

Three main things were in my head while I went downstairs – the CHED chart, Roberto Clemente, and the World Series. The last two things are kind of the same, since Clemente plays for the Pittsburgh Pirates, who are in the World Series right now against Baltimore. Pittsburgh was my first favourite team because I liked the colours of their uniform – white, black and gold. I was thinking about Clemente because I really wanted his baseball card. It's one of the only ones in the 1971 set I don't have, and he's my hero. This year's cards weren't going to be in the stores much longer, so the situation was getting desperate.

The CHED chart, of the top thirty songs on CHED, comes out every week. I've been collecting them since grade one. It's this folded piece of paper, a different colour every week, with a psychedelic design around the edge. One page is the cover, another page has the chart, another one has an ad for a new album. (Last week it was for one by a guy called Bruce Cockburn. I'm not kidding. That's really his name.) The last page has a picture of one of the Good Guys. That's what they call their deejays. I usually always pick up the new chart every Wednesday at Scotty's Records and Tapes at Northgate Mall. This week I was late, and whenever that happens I start to feel all sort of twitchy and nervous. It's hard for me to concentrate on other things. I really need to know who's number one.

I got to the kitchen and Mum was there.

– Morning, Mum, I said.

– Yes, it is, Mum said.

That's a joke me and Mum have. I'll say what time of day it is, and she'll agree with me. Sometimes I say the wrong time of day to make sure she's paying attention.

– Hey, Mum, I said.

– Yaish?

When she says yes like that she's imitating old farmers in Ontario, where she grew up. Most of them didn't have any teeth.

– You walk on a sidewalk, right?

– I suppose.

It was hard to tell if she was really listening. Mum's usually doing something else when she talks to you. She's pretty busy. This time she was making a long list of stuff, I don't know what.

– And you park in a parking lot, right?

– Yaish.

– So how come you don't drive on a driveway?

– Pardon me?

– I mean, you walk on a sidewalk, and you park in a parking lot, so how come you don't drive on a driveway? Okay, you do a bit, but only into the garage, or backwards onto the street. That's not really driving. A driveway is really what they should call a *street*. That's where people drive.

Mum didn't say anything, just kept making her list. I ate my Rice Krispies and brown sugar, and thought about the CHED chart. I predicted to myself that the number one song on the new chart would be 'Do You Know What I Mean?' by Lee Michaels. I'm usually right. I thought Mum must have completely forgot about what I was saying, but then I heard her say something.

– What? I asked.

– I said, the world works in mysterious ways, she said. But it works. People manage to drive and park their cars in more or less the right places, even if the names are confusing. Sometimes it's best just to let the mystery be.

– I guess, I said.

Mr Baldwin, the substitute teacher, told us once that we should always question everything. So Brad Flipchuk asked him why, when there's only nine teams in the CFL, two of them are called the Rough Riders. Somebody else asked why, when old people blow their noses, they always look into the hanky before they put it back in their pocket. What were they looking at? Mr Baldwin said just because you question something it doesn't mean you'll ever know the answer. I think that's the kind of thing Mum was saying too.

Pretty soon it was time to go to school.

– Can I have a dim? I asked Mum.

A dim is ten cents without the e. Mum said once that a dime's not worth a dime any more, so for a joke we made it shorter.

– Just don't spend it all in one place, Mum said, giving it to me.

I ask for a dime about three times a week, and Mum always gives it to me, and she always says that, even though it's practically impossible to spend a dime in more than one place. I think she's thinking about when she was a girl, going with her sisters to the county fair. They'd bob for apples, and eat candy floss, and watch contests where farmboys tried to catch greased pigs. A dime probably lasted them all day.

TWO

Leaving the house, I had to be careful not to let Sam out the back door, because if I did he'd follow me all the way to school. It's happened a few times, and I've had to sit around in class worrying about him all day. Sam used to kill the school's flowers by taking leaks on them. The janitors didn't like it.

Sam's a very loyal dog. He's always taking off, but you know he'll come back. He really gets around, too. One day in the paper there was a picture of this really familiar-looking dog in a part of town we didn't even recognize. This dog was standing around watching some kids play tetherball around a No Parking sign. The caption said 'Enjoying the action is Sam, a neighbour's dog.' Even the newspaper knows his name. Sam's pretty cool, even though he humps the legs of everybody who comes over, and tries to stick his nose up their bums. It's embarrassing.

On the way to school, I thought a bit about what to buy with the dime. The choices were either a pack of baseball cards or a chocolate bar. Me and Keith Puzniak have a thing about trying out new chocolate bars. In grade three there was one called Rum and Butter, and somebody in school started a rumour that there was real rum in it, and that it could get you drunk. Keith believed it.

– It's true, he said. They couldn't call it Rum and Butter if it wasn't real rum. That would be false advertising.

– That's asinine, I said.

Asinine is a word I learned from Bryan Hall, this sports guy on the radio who's always insulting people.

– Is not, said Keith.

He probably didn't even know the word.

– Anyway, he said, I have proof. Me and three other guys ate some and we got drunk.

– What guys? I asked.

– *Other* guys.

– What was it like getting drunk?

– You feel kind of dizzy, and then you puke.

– You really puked?

– We all did.

– How do you know you didn't just puke from eating too much?

– Because, numb nuts. I've seen drunk people. And the puke from getting drunk is a special colour.

– Neat.

I quit arguing, mostly because that was right around the time Keith's dad was fired from his job at the pop bottle factory, and everybody thought it was because he drank too much. And I don't mean too much pop. So Keith probably did know pretty well what happened when people got drunk. I didn't really believe him about the colour of the puke, though.

Maybe it was thinking about how chocolate bars can make you puke that made me decide to buy a pack of cards. I was really close to getting all 550. The trouble is, the closer you get to the end, the harder it is to get the ones left. You end up with, like, thirty of some players, and none of some of your favourites. I've got about a hundred of Coco Laboy, this guy on the Expos who's not even a starter, but I was still looking for Clemente and Rod Carew. I think the card company does it on purpose, to keep you buying packs. It's dumb, too, because you can just order the whole set for thirty bucks, but that sounds like so much. If I added up all the dimes I spend, though, it's probably way more.

I'd get the pack at lunchtime, I thought. Meanwhile I strolled along looking at the election signs on people's lawns. There was an election for mayor of Edmonton coming right up, and there was another one for premier of Alberta a little while ago. Some people still haven't taken those signs down.

Most of the mayor signs said 'Re-Elect Ivor Dent'. He's a guy with wavy silver hair and a funny way of speaking that kind of makes him sound tired. He says he wants to take Edmonton into the twenty-first century by encouraging growth. He's only the mayor because Bill Hawrelak, this really popular guy who's been mayor about five times, keeps getting kicked out for making shady land deals. Dad told me that. Once I heard Dad talking about the election with Otto Pippig, our neighbour across the alley.

– So, who's your horse this time? Dad asked him.

– I don't care about none of these guys, Otto said. Dump 'em in the North Saskatchewan, you ask me.

– What about Dent?

I think Dad liked Dent because he wanted to get an NHL team and the Commonwealth Games for Edmonton. Dad's a huge sports buff.

– What about him? said Otto. Mr Fancy Suit. Sucking up to all those other fancy suits.

– You're not saying bring back Hawrelak?

– I'd have him in a minute.

– He's a thief!

– He's a friend of the working man.

– He should be in jail.

– He could do a better job from jail than any of these —— could do from the Mayor's office.

The blank was some German word that's probably a swear.

Dad gave up and talked about the Eskimos game for a while. Later I heard him muttering, 'I can't believe these people.' I think he was talking about people who kept voting for Hawrelak.

The other signs all said things like 'Now! It's Lougheed' and 'Now! Is the Time for the Progressive Conservatives'. They were from the election where Peter Lougheed, the Conservative guy, beat out Harry Strom, the Social Credit guy. Social Credit was in charge forever in Alberta until Lougheed came along and wiped them out. It was funny looking at their pictures on the signs because Lougheed looked about fifty years younger than Strom, even though they're about the same age. Lougheed's got longer hair with the dry look, and a big smile. Strom still greases his hair back, and instead of smiling he's got this weird look like he's just smelled something bad. Even his name sounds old. You never meet young people called Harry. I'm not surprised he lost, but I feel kind of sorry for all the people who look like him and probably voted for him. You see them leaving the Romanian Centre after Saturday Bingo.

I lived about two and a half Hey Judes from St. Paul's. That Beatles song, which is the longest in the world if you don't count stuff like Beethoven, is seven minutes and fourteen seconds long, so you can figure out how long it takes to walk. I could probably do it in one Hey Jude if I ran.

On the way to St. Paul's, you pass two other schools. There's St. Mary, the junior high, and O'Connor, the high school. All my brothers and sisters except for Mary, who's in grade one, go to those schools. It's weird walking by a school knowing your older brothers and sisters are inside, maybe watching you. You have to be careful not to pick your nose or walk with a girl.

Right across from school I saw Chris Ditka, this guy I've known since grade one who's kind of my friend. I say kind of because, even though we do things together and stuff, I don't really like him. In fact, I can't stand him. He's a hypocrite. All the teachers think he's a great guy but when they're not looking he'll do things like squish your lunch or give you really bad gaunch pulls. One time he pulled Carl Wysocki's gaunch so hard it wouldn't go back down and Carl had to sit with his back to the wall all day to hide it. The one good thing about Chris is he's a big baseball fan, with a card collection even bigger than mine.

– Hey, Neil, you missed a great game, Chris called out.

Yesterday's World Series game, which the Pirates won 2-0, was on in the afternoon, so I couldn't watch. Chris must have skipped school to watch it, and brought a fake note to show his teacher. That's what I mean about him.

– Yeah, I heard about it, I said.

– Nelson Briles tossed a two-hit masterpiece, frustrating the big bats of the Birds, Chris said.

Chris was always memorizing stuff the announcers said and pretending they were his words. Actually, I do that myself sometimes. Dad thinks I should be a sportswriter. I decided to do it now.

– Led by the imperious Clemente, the feisty Bucs are determined to make a series of it.

I'm not even sure what imperious means. Something about having a bad temper.

– Ooh, aren't *we* clever, Chris said.

He doesn't like people doing things that he can do.

– What, is there some law? I asked. Only Chris Ditka may imitate baseball announcers?

Normally I wouldn't bother arguing with Chris. I'm not sure why I did this time. He didn't get mad, though. I was surprised.

Instead, he put his arm around my shoulder, and started talking buddy-buddy.

– Where are we going, pal? he asked.

– To the top, I said.

– What top?

– To the toppermost of the poppermost.

This was a thing we did from that Beatles movie, *A Hard Day's Night*, that we saw at the Romanian Centre when we were about four. We try to do it in Beatle voices.

That kind of got me in a better mood, so we were walking up to the front entrance all happy when right in a flash, Chris stuck a leg in front of me and, at the same time, pushed with the arm that was around my shoulder. I wiped right out, and Chris ran into the school.

– I hope you enjoyed your trip, he yelled.

It's a funny feeling, to be all of a sudden down on the ground when a second before you were just walking along. You notice things you don't usually look at, like gum wrappers and dog turds and the kind of pebbles that are in the cement. When you look up, everything looks gigantic, like it must to babies and insects. So I just sort of stayed there for a minute, imagining I was one of those Lilliput people. Except for some scrapes on my elbows, the trip didn't cause any injuries. I got up and went into school.

THREE

One different thing about grade four is that's when they start
giving you lockers. Having them is neat. You're not always
dragging books around, and you don't have to keep them all in
your desk where they get mixed up with gum wads and cards and
stuff. But it's a problem for some people, who can't remember
how to do their combinations. Carl Wysocki went all day
without books one time because he didn't want to tell anybody
he couldn't figure out his com. He just sat there all day
pretending to write on one piece of paper, and shaking. I felt sort
of sorry for him, but you can't help somebody else with their
com, because then you'd know it.

I got into home room just in time. That's another thing about
grade four. You're not in the same room all the time. You go to
different rooms sometimes, and have classes with different
teachers. That's a bit weird, because before, with the same
teacher all the time, you'd start feeling like she was your mum or
something. So you knew what you could get away with. But now
you see all these different people who get mad at different things.
Some of them can't even remember your name.

My desk was the second to last in the row next to the window.
I picked it on purpose because the room is upstairs, and from it
there's a really good view of O'Connor across the street. When
students there are skipping or on their spares and the weather's
nice, they hang out on a lawn beside the school called 'the
Beach'. They play Frisbee and smoke and neck and stuff. It's fun
to watch. Our teacher, Sister Arlene, doesn't like it too much, but
the principal, Mr Horvath, won't let her shut the blinds because
he's a big believer in the benefits of sunlight. That's what he said.

It's important who you sit next to at the start of the year,
because you end up sitting with them all year. There's no rule
that you have to stay in the same desk. People just do. This year
Victor Nedved sat in front of me. That's a Czechoslovakian
name. I already mentioned his dad, one of the janitors. Mr
Nedved used to be a writer in Czechoslovakia, but the Russians

didn't like what he wrote, so he had to leave. That's what Victor told me. They lived in Praha. That's how they say Prague over there. Victor's got this perfectly round bald spot on the back of his head, about the size of a dime. It's really hard not to put your finger on it.

Brad Flipchuk had the seat behind me. Everybody thinks he must have flunked a couple of times, but he's just huge for grade four. His dad is an undertaker. Those are the guys who make sure you're buried properly when you die. It must be weird having a job where you have to hope people die. Every time I see Brad I think of that song 'War', by Edwin Starr, where he sings how war's only friend is the undertaker. It's a great song.

Beside me in the next row was where Daniela da Silva sat. She must be the richest kid in the school. She's always saying how her dad is an important businessman. Not just a businessman. An important one. She wears dresses like the ones models wear, and her hair, which is practically black, is always pouffed way out like she just came from the hairdresser.

Because I'm interested in geography, and where people are from, I thought I'd ask Daniela that, on the first day of school. I could tell from her accent she was from someplace else, but I couldn't figure out where.

– Where are you from? I asked her.

It seemed to take about five minutes for her to turn her head and look at me, and another five until she said something. When she finally did, it wasn't much.

– Brazil, she said.

– Neat, I said.

She looked at me some more. It was a weird look, like you'd look at somebody who was really bugging you or something.

– Yes, she said. Neat.

She turned again and pretended to be interested in her Duo-Tang. But I wanted to know more.

– So you must speak Brazilian, then, I said. You've got an accent.

Thinking about it now, I know that wasn't a very smart thing to say. But I said it. It was too late to take it back. Daniela, when she heard it, stopped staring into her empty Duo-Tang and turned to look at me, even slower than last time.

– Two things, she said.

I just sat and waited.

– One, she said, I do not 'speak Brazilian'. That would be a very good trick, since there is, in fact, no such language. The language of Brazil happens to be Portuguese. Brazil is, in fact, the largest Portuguese-speaking country in the world.

She stopped and gave me this bug-eyed stare. What made it all worse was, I knew that stuff about what they speak in Brazil. It's in the *Ladybird Book of Flags of the World.* I just forgot. People forget things sometimes.

– Two, Daniela said, it is not especially 'neat' that I am from Brazil. Brazil is not, at this time, a 'neat' place to be.

– What do you mean? I asked.

Just like the last question, this was one I probably shouldn't have asked, at least not right then. But I really wanted to know. All I knew about Brazil was from watching Pele on *Wide World of Sports*, and that song 'The Girl from Ipanema', that's on one of Mum's Herb Alpert albums. Daniela rolled her eyes like she was explaining something to an idiot.

– For your information, she said, Brazil is suffering under a military dictatorship. Many of our most important artists, intellectuals and businessmen have been persecuted or forced abroad.

– Oh, I said.

I almost said 'neat' again. Good thing I didn't. I thought maybe I could make myself look not as stupid by saying some more.

– How can you speak English so well, if Portuguese is what they speak in Brazil? I asked.

She looked like she wouldn't answer, but she did.

– Brazilians, unlike Canadians, are capable of learning other languages, she said. I received an English education in private schools. All my teachers were nuns from Scotland and Ireland.

– Why don't you go to a private school here?

– Because my mother, who incidentally is a French Canadian who went to Brazil to work for the Red Cross, wasn't satisfied with the religious instruction in the private schools here.

– Hey, your mum's from Quebec?

– Yes.

– Neat. I was born in Quebec.

– How utterly fascinating, she said.

One thing about talking to Daniela was that she made me feel, not stupid, but not as smart as her. I always get good report cards, but talking to her I felt a little bit behind for some reason. So that day I decided I'd learn more about Brazil, and try real hard in French, to show her that a Canadian can learn another language. I also have to admit she's pretty good looking.

Not that many other kids in class were people I knew. There was Freddy Livingstone, way over on the other side, who's the only Negro kid I've ever known. There must be only about two Negro families in Edmonton. Freddy's parents are from Trinidad. He's not the friendliest guy in the world, but we were still kind of friends. We liked lots of the same records, like the Jackson Five and Sly and the Family Stone. The only other guy in the class I really knew was Tommy Winchester. He's American. He's got the longest hair I've ever seen on a boy. For the first ever time, Keith Puzniak was in a different class than me this year.

Anyway, after getting into my desk, I was so busy looking out the window and thinking about the World Series that I was a bit late standing up for the Our Father. Lucky for me, Sister Arlene didn't see. The last guy who got caught, Leslie Gibson, got pulled up by his ears. The next recess we all wanted to know what it was like to get pulled up by the ears, so we started doing it to each other, until we realized how much it hurt. Somebody even did it to Leslie again.

As we recited the Our Father, I looked around the room to see how people were saying it. You're not supposed to do that, but it's interesting. Some people don't seem to know the words, and they just sort of mumble along. Some people move their mouths but don't make a sound. Two or three people, like Daniela, say it like they're in a speech contest, all clear and loud. Most people, like me, just mumble along until we get to the parts we know really well, like the 'Amen' part at the end. Those parts we say really loud. It's like saying grace at home. That's this prayer of thanks we say before dinner, usually only when we have guests, which is about once a year. I'm always scared that one day I'll be asked to lead it, because I only know about three words. Everybody rushes through it, and nobody ever actually teaches it to you. They think you're born knowing it or something.

FOUR

The first class of the day was reading. Other years reading was mostly just the teacher reading to the class, books like *Pinocchio* and *Charlotte's Web*, and lots of spelling tests. This year it also includes writing, not just words and sentences but longer stuff. This morning Sister Arlene was talking about what a paragraph is, probably because we just had an essay assignment and most people just wrote one long paragraph, or even one long sentence. I already knew what a paragraph was, though, so I started looking around the classroom and daydreaming.

Up at the front of the room, over the door, there's this sort of X-ray picture of Jesus where you can see right through to his heart. It's the same picture Mum and Dad have in their bedroom. Above the blackboard are pictures of the Queen and her husband. They must be old pictures, because the Queen looks way younger than she does on TV at Christmas, when she gives her message in that weird squeaky voice. Her husband, what's-his-name, always looks the same, and never says anything. In the picture he looks like he's only smiling because the photographer just ordered him to.

I started chipping little pieces of wood around the little hole in the top corner of my desk. Those holes always remind me of my mum's mum, Granny in Harrison's. We call her that because she's from this tiny little town in Ontario called Harrison's Corners. It's just a store and a gas station, with farms all around. The reason the hole makes me think of her is because of a story Mum told me once when I asked her why those holes are there.

– Mum?

– Yaish?

– You know those holes in desks?

– You must mean inkwells.

– Whats?

– Inkwells. In the olden days, when dinosaurs roamed the earth and there were no ballpoint pens, schoolkids would write by dipping a fountain pen into a bottle in the inkwell.

– Did Granny in Harrison's do that?

– Naturally. So did I. And that's not all they were used for.

– What do you mean?

– Well, on a long dull day, the thoughts of a schoolboy may sometimes stray from his lesson. They may stray to the pigtails of the girl in front of him, which hang tantalizingly close to the inkwell.

– Did your pigtails ever get dipped?

– No, although Archie MacDuff probably had designs.

I love it when she says those names. Everybody in the part of Ontario where she comes from has names like Angus McDiddle or Duncan McSomething.

– What about Granny? Did anybody ever do it to her?

– Well, she tells a story about Hughie MacDougall. He was a big farm lad who never really learned to read and write, and he was always tormenting Hilda, until one day.

Hilda is Granny's name. It's another one of those names young people never have.

– Until one day what? I asked.

– Until Hilda had had enough, and turned around and hit Archie square on the forehead with her *McGuffin's English Reader*. At first they thought she'd broken his neck. He was out cold. That was the end of that problem.

– Wow, I said.

As I sat staring out the window, O'Connor and 132nd Avenue turned, in my head, into farm fields around Harrison's, and my classroom became a one-room schoolhouse with an old wood stove in the middle. I was thinking how I'd gather frogs on the way back home, and help out with the harvest, when some change in the air snapped me out of it.

You can tell when something bad's happening in a class because everything goes a special kind of quiet, and that's what was happening now. I looked up to the front of the room and saw Leslie Gibson standing there. His face was turning this weird sort of half-red, half-green colour, and Sister was giving him one of those looks that can put your gaunch in a knot. Somehow, nuns can look way madder than other people. Maybe it's because you can't see their hair or anything, just the mad look on their face. It doesn't help that Sister Arlene is built like a middle linebacker. If she wasn't called Sister you wouldn't even believe she was a

25

woman. She handed Leslie his essay. It was about penguins.

– Mr Gibson, please read the underlined sentence, Sister said.

The room went even quieter. You knew it wouldn't be any ordinary sentence.

– The ability …

– *Louder*, Mr Gibson. Fill the room with your knowledge.

– The ability to withstand intense cold is one of the penguin's main assets.

He said it so fast it sounded like one long word. Nobody made a sound for quite a while. Finally, Sister spoke.

– I have a question for you, Mr Gibson.

– Yes, Sister? said Leslie.

– What, precisely, is an asset?

A bunch of us giggled, because asset sounds so much like ass. But Sister turned around and gave us that look, and it shut us right up.

– I don't know, said Leslie.

– Interesting, then, that you would choose to use it in an essay. With all the richness of the English language, one might have hoped that you would choose a more, shall we say, familiar word.

– Yes, Sister.

I think Leslie was thinking he might be able to sit back down then, but no. Sister kept going.

– I have another question, Mr Gibson.

This definitely wasn't Leslie's day. Most days weren't.

Sister went over to her desk and pulled out a book. I recognized it. It was a volume of *Funk & Wagnall's Encyclopedia*. Almost everybody has them because they get a deal on them at Woodward's Food Floor. If you buy enough groceries, you get a volume free.

– Does this book look familiar, Mr Gibson? Sister asked.

– Yes, Sister, Leslie said.

– Well, it should. It contains a description of penguins uncannily similar to yours. Identical, in fact, except for the words you have managed to misspell.

Normally, this would have been the time for Sister to say something like 'Have you anything to say for yourself, Mr Gibson?', but after looking at him turning the colour of rotten meat, it seemed like even she felt sorry for him. She just asked him to sit down.

– For Mr Gibson, and for anyone else who may entertain notions of such a creative approach to essay writing, I would like to introduce three new words. They may even turn up on your next vocabulary quiz.

Then she turned to the blackboard, and wrote the words in big capitals: PLAGIARISM, SLOTH, DECEIT.

They weren't all new words to me. A sloth is a three-toed animal that sleeps upside down. The other two I looked up in library period. I also looked up 'asset'. The funny thing is, I really learned all those words because of Leslie. Maybe people plagiarizing is a good way to increase your word power.

When Sister finished handing back the essays, I snuck looks at the ones around me. Daniela's was called 'Good Works', probably all about how to be perfect, and of course she got an H, the highest mark. Victor Nedved's was called 'How to Brew Beer', and he got a lousy mark, mostly because he didn't know about paragraphs, and probably also because Sister wasn't too excited about the subject. Brad Flipchuk's was called 'The Art of Undertaking'. I wonder where he got the idea for that one. I couldn't see his mark, but he didn't look too happy about it.

I caught Freddy's eye from across the room, and he mouthed the words 'B Plus', a pretty good mark. I knew about Freddy's essay because I helped him with the spelling. It was called 'Blackbird'. That was my idea. It's the name of a Beatles song. Freddy used it to mean black people, how they're rising and protesting for equality. On all his homework and books Freddy signs the name Clyde. That's the nickname of his hero, a basketball player with the New York Knicks who dresses like the guy in that movie *Bonnie and Clyde*. There was a thing about him in *Life* magazine, with pictures of him hanging out with beautiful women. Freddy says the worst thing about living in Canada is we never get basketball games on TV. He says he's going to move to New York as soon as he graduates. He even knows the year. Nineteen eighty.

I mouthed the words 'H Minus' to Freddy. Sister always found some reason not to give me the highest mark.

The idea for my essay was kind of weird. I was reading a

tourist guide to Expo 67, in Montreal, and I thought, what if there were tourist guides to just ordinary places, like my neighbourhood? So that's what I wrote about. This is it.

A Tourist's Guide to Glengarry

Visitors from around the world will find many sites of interest and beauty in this lovely neighbourhood. Situated in the north part of Edmonton, North America's northernmost metropolis, Glengarry has several schools and playgrounds, a modern shopping centre, and a small drugstore, café, and family grocery store. It is also home to many friendly and colourful characters. Let's look around!

Our tour begins at the home of Joe and Maureen McDonald and their seven children. Their fine split level home is across the street from a public schoolyard and within sight of Northgate Mall, home of Scotty's Records and Tapes. Facing west, the McDonalds have a lovely view of the sunset. Behind the house, a recently paved alley is an excellent place for children to play war games and road hockey. And don't miss Mr Koveleski's crab apple tree, which sticks out over his fence. Yum!

Proceeding east from the McDonalds' back door, we pass the one-story home of the Pippigs, Otto and his lovely wife Elfie. Otto fought in World War II, on the German side. Their back yard was the scene of an unfortunate accident last year when their eight-year-old son Jurgen, running along the boardwalk with one of those plastic fans on a stick in his mouth, tripped. This forced the stick back into his throat, causing a lot of pain and bleeding. Even now, a year later, Jurgen says it hurts when he swallows.

As we continue toward Glengarry's three Catholic schools, we enter an area of row housing, described on a sign as 'affordable'. Here live the Flipchuks, the Nedveds, and other families with sons who go to school with Neil McDonald. In one backyard, you'll see a most impressive birdhouse, with multiple levels and even balconies. Don't talk to the owner, though. He's grumpy and talks only to birds. In German. Oh, and keep an eye out for Sam, the McDonalds' roving dog. He's friendly! Maybe too friendly!

On our left as we approach O'Connor High School is an outdoor hockey rink, used for lacrosse in the summertime. Here you can watch Duncan and Richard McDonald, two of Neil's older brothers, starring for the local community league team. He shoots, he scores!

A sharp right turn takes us onto a path leading to St. Paul's Elementary School. The short green fence on the right is a favourite meeting place for high school students, who enjoy bugging the younger children as they walk by, shouting good-natured remarks and sometimes tripping them. Kids these days!

We could go on, but the charms of Glengarry could fill a book! Why not book your tour today? The topography is flat, the weather is usually nice from about May until October, and the locals are waiting with open arms.

I actually thought it was a pretty good essay. I tried to use the same kind of words they use in tourist books, and I thought it was pretty good to use long ones like 'metropolis' and 'topography'. I thought it deserved an H, but this was Sister's comment:

You write very well, Mr McDonald, but your choice of topic and treatment show a lack of seriousness. Hopefully, you will one day find a theme worthy of your talent.

Probably if I wrote something about helping others, I'd get an H. It's like Freddy's essay. If Sister knew more about what he was writing about, he'd probably get an H, but it's kind of hard to picture her going on a protest march, or sitting around the convent listening to the latest James Brown album.

Just before the end of the class I caught Daniela looking over to see my mark.

She pretends not to care what anybody else does, but you always see her peeking like that.

– Well, she said, it looks like the Nobel Prize committee can rest easy.

At the start of the year, when I said I wanted to write a book some day, just about everybody thought it was a neat idea. Carl Wysocki opened his eyes wide and said 'A book!' Like books were miracles. But Daniela just acts like anybody but her is crazy to try anything that takes brains.

– Oh yeah? I said.

– Yeah, she said.

– What makes you think I can't write a book?

– Well, for one thing, they usually require a vocabulary that includes words of more than one syllable.

I should have shown her 'topography' and 'metropolis', but when I get into an argument I don't always think straight. So I just kept arguing.

– I know lots of big words, I said.

She just sat there tapping her toe.

– What makes you think you're so smart? I asked.

She still just sat there. Finally, she said something.

– I'm still waiting, she said.

– For what?

– For a word of more than one syllable to come tripping from your tongue.

– Why should I say a long word? Just to prove I'm smart? You think you know all the big words in the world?

– You've yet to prove to me that you know any.

– Oh, God, I said.

It was driving me nuts. Some weird part of my brain was forcing me to say one-syllable words, and the harder I tried not to, the harder it got. Finally, I gave up.

– I give up, I said.

– Pardon me?

– I said I give up. You win.

– Win? I wasn't aware there was a competition.

I was about to say something with the word 'dictionary' when the bell rang. I figured I'd get her later. It was time to go down to the library for supervised reading.

FIVE

Going to the library is my favourite thing in school. The only thing that would be better is if there was a class where you sat around listening to records. My sister Susan told me there's a class like that at O'Connor, called Music Appreciation. The teacher is a guy who also plays in a band. He talks about things like how many chords are in a song, and how the more chords there are, the better the song is. I'm not sure what a chord is. The one thing I don't like about the guy is he doesn't like my favourite groups, like the Beatles and Creedence. He says the best band in the world is Chicago, this group with horns. I get this funny excited feeling in my stomach every time I go into a library. Sometimes Mum takes me in the bus to the Centennial Library downtown. The children's library is in the basement. Just inside the door is a glass cage with Iggy the Iguana inside. The librarian says Iggy's more than a hundred years old. He looks totally bored. Also, around the room they have these little white fences with ducks and geese inside. They're not supposed to be able to fly, but one time one of them did. It was really funny, with all these Quiet Please signs around, to watch this goose honking and flapping all over the place, and the librarian trying to catch it without making any noise. Another thing is that the birds are always going to the bathroom in their cages, so the whole room kind of stinks. Sometimes even when you take a book home it still has the smell of duck turds on it. I don't mind, though. It's kind of neat.

Another great place for books is the Bookmobile. It's this giant sort of space-age-looking bus that comes to the neighbourhood about once a month, and you can sign books out. I always thought it would be great to live in it, just driving around staying in campgrounds and reading all the time. If you needed money, you could just sell a few books, and if you got stranded in a cold place, like Saskatchewan in the middle of winter, you could burn books for heat until you got rescued.

I like everything about books, not just reading them but even just holding them and feeling them. If it's a book with shiny paper, I like to run the back of my hand over the page. It gives me goosebumps. If it's an older book, I like to put my nose up close and smell it. If you close your eyes, you can imagine you're in the place the book is from. One time I saw a book from 1924 published in London, England. I sniffed it and closed my eyes and felt like I could see and smell everything there, like in that movie *Oliver*. I also like it when you find people's things between the pages. You'll be flipping through a book and you'll see an old dried booger or a hair, and you think, maybe that came from a famous person. Or you'll see things like old grocery lists or dirty pictures that somebody drew in the margins. The best thing I ever found in a book was an old dollar bill, when it still had a picture of the King of England on it. Dad told me it was too old to spend, but I should save it because it could be worth a lot of money some day. That was about a year ago. I still have it.

The first books I ever read were children's books that were lying around the house. The best were the Dr. Seuss ones. I still love those. You can just sit there and look at the pictures, with all these weird creatures with huge feet and tiny heads, and houses that are flopping over and green skies and blue grass, and after a while you forget about the real world. You stop reading and look around and everything seems so ordinary. One time I saw these hippie guys sitting in front of O'Connor looking at *One Fish, Two Fish, Red Fish, Blue Fish*. They weren't even turning the pages. They just kept staring at the same page for about ten minutes.

The first long book I read all the way through was called *I Play to Win: The Stan Mikita Story*, by Stan Mikita. He tells all about how he was born in a poor village in Czechoslovakia and came to Canada and learned to play hockey. Now he's with the Chicago Black Hawks. At first he was the dirtiest player in the league, but then he started feeling bad about it and the very next year he won the Lady Byng Trophy. That's the one they give to the nicest guy in the NHL. It's a great book. It's neat how sports guys, even when they're playing and practising all the time, can still find the time to write books. Bobby Orr wrote one too. I guess they do it in the summertime.

I read that book about a year ago. Since then I've read tons.

The first one I ever read without pictures was one called *The Pearl*, by John somebody. The subjects I like best are history, geography, sports and wildlife. I would have said music but there aren't that many books about the kind of music I like. Most music books you find are full of notes and stuff. The one time I found a long book about the Beatles it was this stupid thing by some professor guy who kept comparing them to old guys like Beethoven and Mozart. They don't sound anything like that, except on 'Eleanor Rigby', and 'Yesterday'. And one song on *Sgt. Pepper*.

In the library period, everybody's supposed to pick out one book and read it for half an hour. If you can't find a book you like you're allowed to draw or do homework, as long as you don't make any noise. Of course, that's exactly when you feel like making noise. It's like in church. In the parts when you're supposed to be the most quiet, like just before you take the little wafer for communion, those are the times when I think of something like the time this fat lady got stuck in the revolving door at Eaton's. I'll step up to the priest, he'll say 'The Body of Christ', and I'm supposed to say 'Amen', take the wafer in my right hand (which is really hard to remember because I'm left-handed), and put it in my mouth. But all this time I'm killing myself not to laugh out loud right in the priest's face. Mum and Dad wouldn't be too thrilled.

It's easier for me to stay quiet in the library, because I like reading, but for lots of people it's a problem. In grade three Keith Puzniak had this habit of farting in the library. He didn't mean to, but the harder he'd try to hold them in, the more he'd have to blow them. He'd be sitting there, reading a Hardy Boys book or something, keeping his whole body tight so he wouldn't cut one, but sooner or later it would come out, and everybody would giggle. The teacher, Miss Rains, was pretty nice but she couldn't just let this kid sit there farting. It's a small library. So one day she sent him to Mr Horvath's office. Keith came back a bit later looking all relaxed, almost smiling. Later he told me what happened. He got to the office, and right when Mr Horvath was about to ask what the problem was, Keith cut a great big one. Right there in the office. Instead of getting mad, though, Mr Horvath laughed his head off. They sat there chatting for a while, and Keith was dismissed. Just when he was opening the door to leave, he thought he heard a long, low fart. He turned around and Mr Horvath was winking at him.

So I sat there reading while almost everybody else cracked their knuckles or picked their noses. The book I was reading was called *The Horse Who Played Center Field*, by Hal Higdon. It's about this horse who joins a really bad baseball team. Pretty soon they start shooting up to first place because this horse can catch any ball hit to the outfield. He catches them in his mouth. He can't hit very well, though, because he has a hard time holding the bat in his mouth. What I like about the book is that the writer acts like it's perfectly normal for a horse to be playing baseball. It's an ordinary team, in an ordinary city with ordinary fans, but the centre fielder just happens to be a horse. At first people think it's a bit strange, but after a while he's just another player. It must be neat to be a writer, because you can write about real life but if you want to add something completely fake, you can do it, and make it look real. Nobody can tell you not to. Those are the best books, where everything seems real but something unreal is happening.

There was a bit of noise coming from the other side of the room. I looked up and saw a few people standing around Tommy Winchester. They were pretending to be looking for books but really they were sneaking looks at this magazine Tommy always sneaks into class. He'll hide it behind a bigger book and read it all day. It's called *Man, Myth, and Magic*. It's full of pictures of stuff like people getting buried alive in these weird ceremonies and digging themselves up two days later, or bodies that have been frozen in ice for two thousand years and look like they're still alive. There's also pictures I don't like looking at, like ones of this tribe in Africa who get all the young boys together and chop the ends of their things off. It's because of pictures like that that Tommy has to sneak the magazine in. If somebody like Sister Arlene saw it, he'd probably get expelled, but Tommy never seems too worried. He's always got weird, dirty stuff.

I looked past Tommy out the window, and that was when I saw this really weird thing that confused me at first. There's this little park next to the school with a few birch trees (I knew they were birch because Dad taught me how to identify different trees), and I could swear I saw a little kid with an axe trying to chop one down. The axe was practically bigger than him, so he wasn't getting very far, but still it was a pretty strange thing to see.

When I looked a bit closer, I recognized the kid. He was this tiny little guy with dark curly hair named Giuseppe. His parents are the Santuccis, this Italian couple with about eight kids, who run the grocery store on 132nd Avenue. They're always shouting at you in Italian, especially if you're a kid, probably because they've had problems with shoplifting. I kind of like going to their store, because they always have music by those fat opera singers playing, and posters of Rome and Mount Vesuvius on the walls. You feel like you're in Italy.

It was hard not to stare at this tiny kid trying to chop down a huge tree. I noticed that Freddy was looking at him, too. Freddy looked over at me and just shook his head and rolled his eyes. I'm pretty sure we were the only two who saw Giuseppe. A few minutes later we were filing back to home room and Freddy turned around.

– Did you see that? he whispered.

– Yeah, I said.

– Heavy, man. Heavy.

Freddy says 'heavy' a lot, and you can't always tell what he means. So I asked him.

– What do you mean? I asked.

– What I mean is, we've just seen a perfect example of man's disrespect for mother nature. Man, that kind of thing gets me mad. The little man was way out of line.

Freddy talks just like his dad, who I met once. His dad always says 'Little man, you're way out of line' to him.

– What do you think we should do? I asked.

– Not much we *can* do, man. But that's okay. Instant karma's gonna get him. Heavy.

Freddy was using a line from a song by John Lennon. Karma is this idea where if you do something bad, sooner or later you'll pay for it, later in your life or after you're reincarnated. (I read that in *Man, Myth and Magic*). For example, even if Giuseppe didn't get caught chopping down the tree, he'd get punished by coming back in a later life as a tree. He'd have to just stand there, with dogs peeing on him, or lightning striking him, or maybe even some other little kid chopping him down, and there's nothing he could do about it.

As we were walking down the hall another grade four class came the other way. This was the one with Chris Ditka in it. Just as he passed he flashed a baseball card at me. It was Roberto Clemente, the card I needed more than any other. Chris knew that, so he was always torturing me with it, demanding ten other cards in a trade, or just happening to look at it when he knew I was around. I never should have told him I needed it, because he's one of those people who'll find out what you want and try to make sure you don't get it, just to make himself feel big. Another thing that bugs me about Chris is that he's got really short hair, almost a brush cut. I've noticed that most of the people I like have longer hair, and people I can't stand have shorter hair. I don't know why that is.

SIX

I got back to home room feeling kind of funny, mostly because of the Clemente card. When there's something you really want, and you know it's really close but you can't get it, it's hard to concentrate on anything else. The priest in church said once that 'The Kingdom of Heaven is within'. That means it doesn't really matter what you have, as long as you're a good person. It's like those Indian guru guys you see in *National Geographic*. They train themselves not to need anything, hardly any food even, and they live in a cave or under a tree just thinking about God all day, but they're happy. They're probably not worrying about baseball cards. I wish I could be more like them, but I can't help it.

Thinking about wanting stuff, and wishing you could have what somebody else has, reminded me of my old friend Jimmy Letendre, who moved away in grade one. Jimmy and me used to go around all the back alleys in the neighbourhood, pretending we were explorers, or just hanging out. One day, as we were walking on the path next to the Pippigs' place, we both saw this reflection on the ground, like the sun off a piece of glass. I was so busy thinking about how neat it looked that I didn't try to pick it up, but Jimmy seemed to know something right away, and he dived for it. He picked the thing up and started screaming.

– A quarter! A quarter!

– Let me see, I said.

He held out his hand but not too close.

– Can I hold it? I asked.

It sounds weird but I'd never actually held a quarter before, only dimes and nickels.

– No way, Jimmy said. It's mine.

– I didn't say I *wanted* it. I just want to *hold* it for a sec.

– No way, no way, he kept saying.

He was acting like a quarter was a million dollars. Actually, it was a lot of money in those days. You could buy five chocolate bars with one. But what bugged me was that finding it seemed to turn Jimmy into a different person. He had this wild look in his eyes, and I don't think he even heard what I was saying. He was just thinking about what he could buy, and in a minute he was running off to Santucci's store like I wasn't even there.

The point of my story is, it still bugs me now, three years later, that I didn't dive for that quarter first. Even though I've had quarters since then, and even though I would have finished the five chocolate bars in an hour, I still wish I could go back in time and grab that quarter. It's stupid, because Jimmy was from a really poor family and a quarter was a very big deal to him. If I was a really nice guy, I would have given him the quarter even if I'd got it first, but I know deep down that I would have kept it. Every time I walk by the spot where we found it, and that's every day, this little jealous feeling comes back, like the feeling when Chris showed me his Clemente. It's weird knowing what you feel is wrong, but feeling it anyway.

It was time for recess then, so we put our books in our lockers and went outside. I kept hanging out with Freddy. It's interesting being around him, because you can watch how different people act around a Negro person. You're always hearing about prejudice against black people in the States, people calling people nigger and those guys in ghost sheets burning crosses, but Freddy doesn't really have problems like that. Everybody stares at him, but I think it's just because he looks so different. They stare like they'd stare at some new insect. The first time I saw Freddy, a bunch of kids at the playground were asking him about his hair.

– How do you get it like that? one girl asked.

Freddy's hair is one of those big round afros.

– You don't *get* it like this, Freddy said.

– What do you mean? another kid asked.

– What I mean is, it just *goes* like this. It's a natural.

– Do you comb it?

– Yeah, but not like what you think. I use a pick.

He pulled out this big plastic thing and stuck it in his hair. It just stayed there. Pretty soon everybody was feeling his hair, asking if they could stick things like pencils and crayons in it. Freddy just kind of rolled his eyes, like parents when their kids are doing something stupid. That's when I thought of something I thought would impress him. I tried it.

– Say it loud, I said.

I was thinking of this James Brown song I heard once, called 'Say It Loud, I'm Black and I'm Proud'.

– Say *what* loud? somebody asked.

They were all looking at me like I was a Martian. Freddy smiled, though. He knew what I was talking about.

– I'm black and I'm proud, he said.

In a minute all the other kids left, and it was just me and Freddy.

– Hey, Freddy, can I ask you something? I asked.

– Shoot, he said.

– Black people have afros to show they're proud, right?

– Right on, he said.

– So how come James Brown doesn't have an afro?

– Yes he does.

– No he doesn't. I saw him on Ed Sullivan. His hair's all kind of slicked back and shiny. It looks like some weird helmet.

Freddy was getting annoyed, I think because he knew I was right.

– I don't know, man. Maybe the brother's hair just don't *go* natural. The cat's still Soul Brother Number One.

– Hey, I didn't mean to start a fight. I just thought it was weird that he didn't have an afro. It's no big deal.

– Whatever, man. Anyway, Sly's my man now.

I knew who he meant. Sly and the Family Stone. 'Everyday People' was one of the first records I ever bought. They're really wild looking, all black and white and men and women together, and their music's kind of like the Beatles but more dancy.

– Sly's got a great big afro, I said.

– Damn right he does, Freddy said.

So we talked for a while about our favourite Sly records. We got to be pretty good friends after that, as good as Freddy gets with anybody. He mostly just likes being by himself.

When we got outside for recess, we met Keith Puzniak. This was the first year I wasn't in the same class as Keith, so mostly the only times I saw him were at recess or on the way to or from school.

– Watching the game tonight? Keith asked me.

He always just starts talking to you without saying hi or anything. I do it too.

– Yeah, I said.

Tonight was a big deal because it was going to be the first night game in World Series history. That meant we could see the whole game.

I started to tell Keith about Chris bugging me with the Clemente card. Keith understood, but Freddy interrupted.

– What's with this cat anyway, man? Freddy asked.

– What cat? Chris? I asked.

– No, not that turkey. I'm talking about this baseball cat you're always talking about.

– Clemente?

– Yeah, whatever. What's the big deal about this cat?

It's hard to explain why somebody is your hero. I mean, I could tell stories about Clemente, but unless you're a baseball fan, and Freddy's not, you wouldn't really get them. Like this time I was watching an Expos game and Clemente hit a homer, and his next time up, the pitcher tried to bean him. Most players would scream something at the pitcher or charge the mound or just whine to the ump, but all Clemente did was step out of the box and just stand there and stare at the pitcher for a minute, with this really calm but scary look in his eyes. They showed the pitcher and he looked like he was about to apologize or start crying. That was so neat. Another cool thing Clemente did was, when sportswriters would call him Bob, he wouldn't even answer them. This went on for years. 'My name is Roberto,' he'd say. Finally the writers had to stop calling him Bob. They had no choice.

– I don't know, I said. He's just a real cool guy. He makes people call him his real name.

– Wow, man, said Freddy. Heavy.

I'm not sure he really meant it, though. I didn't do a very good job of explaining. In a minute Freddy wandered off, and it was just me and Keith.

The schoolyard where we spend recess has two main parts. There's the cement part by the school, and the grass part with portables and soccer goalposts. Most of the girls play on the cement part. They do stuff like skipping ropes and playing hopscotch, and lots of them just stand around in little groups.

It's weird about girls. They're supposed to be all soft and nice, but you always see them making fun of other girls. They'll pick out one girl who's shy or different, and be really nasty to her. For example, there's Judy. Her mum is a waitress in Woodward's restaurant. Judy always looks kind of sloppy, with her hair all in tangles and her leotards slipping down, and she drags her feet when she walks. The other girls are always singing mean songs to her, and not letting her play with them. The only girl who doesn't do that is Daniela. She just ignores everybody and reads a book or something.

The boys all play out on the grass. Before the snow falls it's usually soccer or touch football, and in winter it's marbles or snowball wars. Last winter there was tons of snow, and the snowplough left these big piles in the schoolyard. Pretty soon there were these big contests to see who could control the piles. The biggest guys, like the grade sixes, would get on top and protect their pile by throwing snowballs and shoving people back down. It started getting pretty violent. It was great. Everybody was wearing those winter masks that hide your face, so nobody knew who anybody was. You could do stuff you wouldn't normally do. I was running around shoving guys way bigger than me, and nailing guys with really hard snowballs. The mask made me feel invincible, until somebody, I think it was Brad Flipchuk, nailed me and I got a nosebleed. My blood was all over the snow. It looked really neat. The next day they made a PA announcement that the piles were off limits. They put that yellow tape, like police use, around them.

Walking around, we noticed that a bunch of the grade threes were looking at shiny new books. It must have been the new Scholastic Books shipment. In grade three everybody joins this book club, where you pick books from a little catalogue and about a month later a box full of them comes. I used to get so excited the night before they came that I couldn't sleep. When the teacher pulled out the box, we'd all practically kill each other to get at the books. The most popular one was this science book that included a free magnet. It was just this tiny thing, taped to the inside back cover, but we all acted like it was something from outer space, and we all did experiments with it, like pulling a long string of pins. Later we did weirder experiments, like seeing if you could pull down your fly with it. Pretty soon it got kind of boring, so it was funny to see the grade threes getting excited just like we did.

It's kind of sad, when you think about it, how something that was fun can all of a sudden be stupid. It's like this thing me and Keith used to do at Northgate Mall. We'd buy these malts that were in Styrofoam cups, and when we finished them, we'd turn the cups upside down and stomp on them. There's lots of echo in the mall, so they'd make a sound like a nuclear explosion. One day last summer we were there, and Keith did it, and it scared the head off this old lady. Keith thought it was a riot, but for the first time, I didn't think it was funny. I felt kind of bad for the old lady. Maybe she was in the war or something, and it reminded her of a bomb. I wanted to tell her I was sorry, but I didn't.

There were a few small soccer games going on at recess, but we didn't feel like playing, so we just kept bumming around. I liked the way things looked, with all the gold leaves flying around, and the grass turning brown. Then I remembered something I wanted to ask Keith.

– Who was that old lady I saw you with? I asked.

A couple of days before, I saw Keith sitting on his front step with this lady who looked like she stepped out of an old book. She was almost totally round, and she was wearing this baggy black dress with one of those kerchiefs on her head.

– That was my baba, Keith said.

– Your what?

– Baba. It's Ukrainian for grandma. She's my mum's mum.

– Why does she dress like that?

– I don't know. Ask her. That's just the way they dress out there.

– Out where?

– Out on the acreage. She lives on this farm by Vegreville, with about a million other old Ukrainian people. They all dress like that.

I remembered once driving past Vegreville. We were on our way to see our cousins in Cold Lake, and we passed some fields with old people out working in them. They must have been Ukrainians.

– What were you talking about with her? I asked

– Not much. She doesn't really know English.

– Do you know Ukrainian?

– Not really.

– So how can you talk with her?

– I don't know. She just sits there talking Ukrainian, and I pretend I understand. You can figure some of it out by the way she says it. Usually my mum tells me later what she was saying.

– So what was she saying when I saw you guys?

– I don't know. My mum wasn't there.

Ever since Mr Puzniak got fired, Mrs Puzniak's been working at two jobs, so she's not around much. That was probably why the baba was there. I was thinking about other things to ask Keith when the buzzer rang and everybody stampeded back inside. It must be weird having grandparents who are totally different from you. My grandparents in Ontario are kind of different. They have funny accents and say things like 'Heavens to Betsy!' but I can usually understand them. Aunt Mary Janet, who's about ninety-eight, I can't understand at all. She has no teeth, and when she talks she just makes this funny sort of rattling sound. You have to pretend you know what she's talking about.

SEVEN

The class after recess was gym. They made a new rule this year that you couldn't wear fancy shoes on the gym floor. Most people in our class already wore running shoes, so they didn't have to worry about changing. Two or three big shots, like Daniela, always brought runners they could change into. It's funny to see her running around in a fancy dress and leotards but with these big red Converse All-Stars on her feet. Some people, like me, wear Hush Puppies, which are pretty close to runners but make really loud squeaking sounds and keep falling off. And some people, like Leslie Gibson, have mums who make them wear fancy shoes to school but don't have runners, so they have to run around in their sock feet. Of course, those are the people who always get stomped.

Our gym teacher this year was Mr Newcombe. He's from Australia. All the girls think he's great because he's got a body like a weightlifter, and he wears these tight little shorts and an undershirt. There's really no reason for him to dress like that, because all he really does is stand around yelling at people, things like 'Look sharp!' and 'Head up!', 'Good show!' or 'Bad show!' He decided he liked me at the start of the year because I'm a pretty good free throw shooter in basketball. Every time he'd see me sink a shot he'd yell out, 'Montreal! 1976!' That's where the Olympics are going to be that year. He never stopped to figure out that I'll only be fourteen in 1976. The only way I could go to the Olympics is if I was one of those tiny female gymnasts. Maybe Daniela will go.

Another thing that bugs me about Mr Newcombe is that his accent reminds me of when I almost died. The one time I took swimming lessons was about two years ago, and the instructor was another Australian guy, or maybe from New Zealand. I showed up late for class and I was so nervous I couldn't think, partly because I'm scared of water, and partly because my trunks were too big and they kept slipping down. I ended up joining the wrong level group, people who could already swim a bit, and who were bigger than me.

That day's lesson was the dead man's float, where you just kind of lie on your stomach with your arms hanging. One by one, everyone was jumping in the pool and doing it, and the coach kept yelling 'Jolly good! Jolly good!' As my turn kept getting closer, I looked over to the other side of the pool, where the group I was supposed to be in were learning to get their toes wet or something. But I was too chicken to say anything. Finally, it got to my turn. The coach looked at his list of names.

– You must be new, mate, he said. I don't see you here.

– My name's Neil.

– Well, jolly good, Neil! In you go!

What else could I do? I jumped in. The only other time I was in a pool was in the shallow end, where your feet can touch the bottom when your head's still not under. But this time it was way deeper. My feet just kept going, and I closed my mouth too late and swallowed a bunch of water. I panicked and started thrashing around. Somehow, I got my head back up, but there was too much water in my mouth to scream for help. I wanted the coach to pull me out, but he just kept yelling.

– Jolly good! Great work, lad! Keep your arse up and your head down!

I sank again, and I could just see his face all wavy above me, still yelling at me. It got harder and harder to move. I figured out to keep my mouth closed, but now there was water all up my nose and I felt like my head would explode. By some miracle, when I hit the bottom I managed to spring back up to the top. Coach started to yell 'Jolly good!' again, until somebody else elbowed him, and they pulled me out. After that, I think I passed out for a while. Maybe they did that thing where somebody pushes on your stomach and water comes shooting out your mouth. The first thing I saw when I woke back up by the side of the pool was the coach's face looking down at me.

– That's the trouper, he said. A real little fish. Good on ya, mate! Jolly good!

I never went to another swimming lesson, and ever since then, whenever I hear an Australian accent, like Mr Newcombe, or on that show Skippy the Bush Kangaroo, that old feeling of drowning while some guy yells 'Jolly good!' comes back.

Today we were playing dodgeball, this game where three big

soft rubber balls get thrown around. The idea is to not get hit. If you do, you drop out. Also, you can't run with the ball, so you have to throw it from the place where you pick it up. It gets harder as more people drop out. A couple of times playing dodgeball, I've tried to use this method I saw once on *Wide World of Sports*. These Japanese kung fu masters could concentrate so hard that they knew everything that was going on around them, even with their eyes closed. They'd be sitting there blindfolded, and a kung fu student would come diving at them, really quietly, from behind. The master would just move a few inches and the other guy would go flying into a wall or something. So I'd stand in the middle of the gym, concentrating my head off, but in about five seconds I'd get nailed by somebody. I figured out that the best method for me was to run around a lot. And try to keep my back to the wall.

Most people get hit right away, because they're too slow or uncoordinated to get out of the way. A few people, like Tommy Winchester and Freddy, get hit on purpose because they think the whole thing is boring and stupid. I like it, though. Pretty soon, there were only three people left – me, Daniela, and Brad Flipchuk. Daniela does this thing where she hides for most of the game and then tries to surprise people. I was ready for her, though, and when she threw the ball at me I caught it, which doesn't count as a hit. So there she was, standing just a few feet away, and me with the ball raised above my head.

– Hey, Daniela! I yelled. How many syllables in *this*?

And I drilled her. It felt so good that I forgot for a minute about Brad. I turned around just in time to see a ball coming straight for my forehead, and before I could move it bounced off me almost all the way to the ceiling. Brad was the winner. There's supposed to be a no hits above the shoulders rule, but Mr Newcombe was laughing like a madman, so he obviously wasn't going to disqualify Brad. Actually, I'd rather get hit in the head than on my thing, which happened once. That's the worst pain I've ever felt.

EIGHT

When we got back to home room, it was funny to be sitting right
by Brad and Daniela. Brad was all braggy because he'd hit me, but
I didn't care because I was so happy about hitting Daniela. She
was pretending not to care, but you could tell she did.

– I hope you enjoy your little moment in the sun, she said.
Because the last time I checked, dodgeball was not one of the
qualifying subjects for university. Some of us prefer to dedicate
ourselves to higher things.

– Yeah, right, I said. Like I practise dodgeball all the time. You
just can't stand losing.

– We'll just see who comes out the winner in the game of life.
Twenty years from now, when I'm a famous neurologist, you'll be
an overweight dodgeball coach.

– What's a neurologist?

– You wouldn't understand, she said.

– No, really. What is one?

I wasn't trying to bug her. I was just interested. She gave me
that how stupid can you get look, but at the same time, she was
turning all red. I really don't think she knew what a neurologist
was. I dropped it.

By this time, the next class was starting. It was French. This
is the first year grade fours have had it. Mum says we're lucky,
because people who know French will get all the best jobs in the
future. Canada will be totally bilingual. I think learning French is
neat for two reasons. One is because I was born in Quebec. I have
a French birth certificate and everything. We moved to Edmonton
when I was about six months old, and we're a totally English
family, but I still like to think I'm part French, even though we
were only living in Hull because Dad was working in Ottawa, for
the Canadian Wildlife Service. The other reason is the French
channel on TV, CBXFT. They show lots of Expos and Canadiens
games you don't get on the two English channels. It's fun learning
the French words for things like strike and puck. You can use
words in road hockey by yelling things like 'Passez-moi

l'hirondelle!' or, if it's winter and there's no real puck, 'Passez-moi le merde du chien!' I love it when the announcer at the Montreal Forum does the three stars. 'La troisième étoile, da turd star, Yvan Cournoyer!!' Also, the French channel sometimes shows dirty late movies. I've never stayed up for one, but some day I will.

Our teacher was Monsieur Houle, a real French guy from Quebec. Dad said we were lucky, because Trudeau put French in the schools so fast that a lot of the teachers don't even know it. They just have to try to know a bit more than the students. Monsieur Houle knows everything, though. For example, on the first day, he was telling us (in English) how you use different muscles in your mouth when you speak French. Your tongue and lips go a different way. I didn't believe him, but later I watched the French channel with the sound off, and he was right. Everybody's lips looked like they were getting ready for a kiss. It was really funny. The trouble is, if you think too much about your mouth muscles and lips while you're talking, you end up choking or drooling.

Monsieur Houle likes to talk about growing up in Quebec, collecting maple syrup from trees and going to the winter carnival in Quebec City. He taught us that song, 'Mon Pays', that they call the national anthem in Quebec. It always reminds me of that FLQ stuff that happened last year. Our family was sitting around watching TV, *Front Page Challenge* or something, when the screen went blank and one of those special bulletin things came on. Mum said the only other time she remembered that happening was when John F. Kennedy was shot, so we knew it would be something big. Lloyd Robertson came on and started talking about these guys, the FLQ, who want to separate from Canada, so they kidnapped this British guy and locked him in the trunk of a car. They wouldn't let him out. Later, Trudeau sent tanks all through the streets of Montreal. It was really exciting. That kind of thing usually only happens in the States or in Ireland.

I was in Montreal once, when I was seven. We went to see Man and His World, which used to be Expo 67. All I really remember is all these freeway overpasses shooting all over the place, and Dad couldn't read the French signs. If you got on the wrong ramp, you couldn't get off. You'd end up way out in the country somewhere. Dad hates traffic anyway. He parks as far away from things as he can. Sometimes on Sundays, he parks closer to home than to church.

Some people like French class, and some people don't. Daniela's great at it because her mum speaks French, and also because it's close to Portuguese. Brad tries hard because he wants to play for the Canadiens some day. He thinks you have to pass some French test to get on the team. Victor Nedved hates it, though. He thinks it's a sissy-sounding language. He lived in France for a while, after his family escaped from Czechoslovakia, and he didn't have a very good time there. He can't understand why he has to learn French here. Whenever he has to answer a question he does it in a girly voice, and everybody laughs. Actually, everybody laughs all the time in French class, especially at words like *pu*, which is the past tense of something.

Today, we were learning a song called 'Un Eléphant sur Mon Balcon', about a guy who finds an elephant on his balcony. It's a pretty feeble song. I'd rather learn the French part of 'Michelle', that Beatles song. There's another one on the radio, not by the Beatles, called 'Ma Belle Amie'. I'd like to learn what that one means, too. I think music is a good way to learn a new language. If I was an English teacher, I'd play songs that had lots of words but music that wasn't too loud, like by that Bob Dylan guy, or maybe Gordon Lightfoot. It would be neat to be off in Africa somewhere, playing records for some tribe, like that one I saw on a *National Geographic* special that talks by making little clicking noises with their tongues. They could teach me how to do that.

The one thing I don't like about Monsieur Houle is that he has a big problem with long hair on boys. It's dumb, because his hair is all slicked up Elvis style, and if he just let it hang it would probably go all the way down to his waist. He'll walk around the room, tugging on the ends of guys' hair. The only word I can understand him saying is *'cheveux'*, which means hair, but you can tell he's making fun of us. Me and Tommy Winchester get it the worst, because we've got the longest hair out of all the boys. The weird thing is that Freddy, with his gigantic afro, never gets bugged at all. I don't think Monsieur Houle knows what to say about afros.

49

Hair is weird. It's not like you grow it like you grow flowers or something. It just ends up long. Me and my brothers have long hair, partly because Mum is too busy to be cutting it all the time, and partly because all the best bands have it. Try naming a good band with brushcuts. You can't. Also, the longer a band's hair gets, the better their music gets. If you look at all the Beatles album covers, it keeps getting longer. On *Sgt. Pepper*, for the first time, they've all even got moustaches, and everybody says that's their best album. On the cover of *Hey Jude*, John Lennon's beard is so big you can barely see his face, and that album's got great songs like 'Rain' and 'Revolution'.

When all our family gets together, like at church or in the station wagon to go on a trip, people really stare at us, and I'm pretty sure it's because of our hair. To see four boys with long hair, and three girls with wild clothes, with normal-looking parents, must be strange for some people. Once two of Susan's friends told me I looked like Brian Jones, the blond guy in the Rolling Stones. I looked at an album cover and our haircut was kind of the same, but his face was all puffy and sick looking. Susan told me that was just before he died of drugs.

The most hair I ever saw in one place was two years ago, when we were down east to see our relatives. Most of them are on farms in Ontario, but two of them, Uncle Mike and Aunt Sheila, are in New York State. One day we drove down from Cornwall to see them in Saranac Lake, where they live. I was all excited because it was my first time in the States. We were passing little general stores with American flags flying in front, and funny little gas stations with front porches and names like Charlie's Gas.

After a while, we started noticing that there was more and more traffic, until there was so much we could hardly move. There were cars as far as you could see down the highway. That was strange enough, but the really weird thing was that everybody, all the drivers and all the passengers, people in big fancy cars and in tiny Volkswagens, had really long hair. I'd heard about hippies before, and seen pictures in *Life* magazine, but we didn't have very many in Edmonton. To be all of a sudden surrounded by them was cool but kind of scary too. We just kind of sat there, with our faces pressed against the windows of the station wagon. There were people with painted faces, girls wearing hardly anything, and a big school bus covered with psychedelic paint and people sitting with guitars on the roof. When we finally got to Saranac Lake, they were everywhere, in sleeping bags and pup tents on people's lawns, even a motorcycle gang cruising around on those great big choppers. Uncle Mike and Aunt Sheila were standing on their porch looking pretty shocked, like their town was being taken over by space aliens. They said something about a big music concert that was happening thirty miles away. The people here were the ones who couldn't make it all the way, because the crowds were too big.

Mum and Dad weren't too sure about letting us out of the house, but Susan said we'd be careful, and we walked around the town. Everywhere we went, people would give us the peace sign, or just smile at us. Some of them held out these funny-smelling cigarettes to Susan. I know now that they were marijuana. People who lived in the town were making money by renting out their front lawns and selling sandwiches and Kool-Aid, but for pretty cheap. It was funny to see ladies who looked like Mum chatting and laughing with guys in Hell's Angels jackets. Nothing bad happened for the two days we were there. Sometimes now, we still talk about it, and it's like this really neat dream we all had at the same time. It's almost like it never really happened.

About a year later, when an album and a movie called *Woodstock* came out, it hit me. That was the concert all those hippies were trying to get to! I remembered, while we were trying to sleep in Uncle Mike's attic, hearing, or thinking I heard, this sort of faraway thumping sound. That must have been the actual music from the concert! As I looked at the names on the album cover at Scotty's Records and Tapes, I couldn't believe all the bands who'd been there. The Who, Sly and the Family Stone, Santana, Jimi Hendrix. They're all favourites of mine, but the weird thing was, I didn't even know who they were two years ago. Maybe the concert sort of seeped into my brain, and made me like them. It drives me a bit nuts to know I was that close to seeing them, and some of them, like Hendrix, are dead now and I won't get the chance. It's not fair.

It's a pretty sure thing Monsieur Houle wasn't at Woodstock, but he's still not a bad teacher. Today we went up and down the rows, saying stuff like 'Comment t'appelles-tu?' and 'J'ai mal à la tête!' then saw some slides of the teacher's holiday in Paris, until the lunchtime bell rang. I looked over at Daniela to see if she was noticing how fast I was learning French, but I couldn't tell.

On my way out of the room, something really weird happened. Monsieur Houle came up to me, put his hand on my shoulder, and said 'Bonne chance, Neil', and something else in French. 'Bonne chance' means good luck. What was he talking about, anyway? Good luck with what? Eating my lunch? Getting home safely? Completing my baseball card collection? I didn't get it, but I didn't think about it too much.

NINE

As all the classes were pouring out for lunch, I saw my sister Mary with a bunch of grade ones. I know she saw me, too, but we didn't say hi or anything. You just don't do that. People in different grades, and especially brothers or sisters from the same family, never have anything to do with each other in school or in the playground. Once you're a block or so away, it's different. You can talk and stuff. But not before. Don't ask me why.

I bumped into Keith by the door, and we started walking home together. If we walk fast, there's just enough time to eat a sandwich, watch *The Flintstones*, and get back by 1:00, but today we didn't feel like hurrying. We just walked along, kicking rocks and chatting.

– Did you see Giuseppe Santucci with the axe? I asked.

– What? said Keith.

– This morning. It looked like he was trying to chop down one of those trees over there.

I pointed over to the park. The tree was still there.

– Giuseppe? Keith said. He's not even big enough to pick up an axe.

– I swear, I saw him. Freddy did too.

– So?

– What do you mean, *so*? He can't do that.

– Why not?

– Well, what if little kids were walking around with axes everywhere? What would happen then?

– I don't know.

– You don't know? It's not safe!

– Look, it's not gonna happen anyway, so why go mental about it?

It was hard getting Keith excited about anything. He'd been that way about everything lately, even the World Series, which he was nuts about last year when Baltimore won. So I changed the subject.

– Tell me more about your baba, I said.

53

– What do you want to know? Keith asked.

At least he was talking.

– I don't know, I said. When did she come to Canada?

– Mum told me they came in the thirties.

He meant the 1930s. They called them the Dirty Thirties. We learned that in enterprise class.

– So she's been here for, like, forty years, and she still can't speak English? I asked.

– I told you, Keith said. She lives with other Ukrainians. They don't need to know English.

– But how can she do stuff like read the paper?

I realized as soon as I asked that it was a stupid question. I do that sometimes.

– Here's the story, genius, Keith said. She can't read anyway, not even in Ukrainian. Everything she needs to know, she remembers. And even if she could read, what do you think they do out there on the farms, sit around checking the hockey scores and reading the comics? They work. The women work at home, the men work out in the fields, and when it's really busy, everybody works out in the fields.

– What do they do for fun?

– I don't think they have much fun. There's not enough time. Some of them paint Easter eggs, and do these weird folk dances. That's about it. I asked my dad about that once, his parents' hobbies, when they were young. He said there's not much time for hobbies when you're living in a hole in the ground.

– In a what?

– It's true. When they first came here, they got off at the train station in Edmonton, and they had to walk about two hundred miles to get to their land. There's no house when you get there, it's just land. So you live in a dirt house until you can build a real one. The thing was, winter came before they could even build a dirt house, so they had to live in the hole they dug the dirt from. Lots of people did it.

– They *lived*? In a *hole*?

– Yeah. It wasn't as bad as it sounds.

– What did they have for a roof?

– I don't know. Branches and grass and stuff.

– Weren't there worms and stuff?

– It was winter, fart face. Anyway, a few worms never killed anybody.

– Did they keep their stuff in boxes, or on shelves, or what? What did they sleep on?

– Look, I don't know all the details. They didn't exactly have a lot of stuff to keep in anything. What do you think, they walked two hundred miles with a bunch of books and china or something? And they probably made some kind of straw bed to sleep on. They knew they'd only be in the hole until winter was over, so they didn't try to turn it into a mansion or anything.

I was dying to know how they went to the bathroom, but I could tell Keith was getting a bit tired of my questions, so I didn't ask. Probably they had another, smaller hole that they went in.

By this time, we were at Santucci's store, where we always stop off, so I stopped thinking about people in holes. Even when you don't have money to spend, it's always fun to go in Santucci's, hang out a bit and maybe hear Mr Santucci singing opera. Today I actually had a dime, so it was even better. When we got in, we saw that Chris Ditka was in there too, trying to decide if he should get six packs of baseball cards or just four. He's always got tons of money. He says it's because he does a paper route, but sometimes I wonder. Last year Freddy said he saw Chris opening one of those little UNICEF boxes that you take around on Halloween. There's no reason to open them. You're just supposed to hand the box in full of money. So you can see why I'm suspicious of Chris. I walked up to him.

– Hey, Chris, I said. Wanna trade?

– You're always asking me that, he said.

– Well, do you?

– But you've got nothing I need.

– I've got Alex Johnson, and Manny Sanguillen.

– Yeah, well, I'm getting six packs. They're gonna be in them this time.

– Wouldn't it be easier just to trade me some of your doubles, than to keep buying a zillion packs? I asked.

– Doubles? What are you talking about, doubles? I don't have any.

– What do you do with your extra cards, then?

– I throw them out! What use are they, anyway?

It was useless trying to explain to Chris that you could trade your extras for players you didn't have. If he hadn't figured that out by now, he was never going to. Besides, I could never just throw out a card, even one I had ten of. I like cards too much.

– So, I guess you don't want to make a deal for Clemente, I said.

– I guess not.

I gave up talking to Chris. Me and Keith chose what we wanted to get – me a pack of cards, Keith a Coffee Crisp. We were standing behind Chris for a while, waiting to pay for our stuff, listening to the opera music.

Then, as Chris was leaving the store, we both noticed something. Chris had four packs in his hand, and one pack sticking out of each back pocket of his jeans. We looked at the number on the cash register. Forty cents. That meant Chris stole two packs! He must have known that when Mr Santucci was wearing his reading glasses to ring stuff up, he can't see more than a few inches, so there was no way he'd see the packs in the pockets. Me and Keith gave each other this spooked look. We were both too shocked to say anything. We must have stood there for a while, because Mr Santucci started getting all impatient.

– You gonna buy that stuff, or what? he said. I don't got all day, you know.

So we paid for our stuff, but I hung around. I felt like I had to say something. Keith got tired of waiting, said he'd see me at school, and left.

I stood there, pretending to look at some mojos or something, but really trying to think of the best way to squeal on Chris. It was hard, because I'd never squealed on anybody before. It's something you just don't do. Even if somebody's been cheating at marbles, or being dirty in road hockey, you always try to sort things out without going running to some adult. Nobody likes a squealer, but this seemed different somehow.

– You want somethin' else? Mr Santucci asked.

You could tell it was getting on his nerves, seeing this kid just standing there.

– No, I said.

– You got somethin' to say?

– Yeah, I said.

– Wella spit it out. I'm busy.

It was do or die. If I didn't squeal on Chris now, I never would.

– What part of Italy are you from? I asked.

Mr Santucci looked at me, and I looked at him. There was no sound for a minute, not even on the opera tape. Have you ever heard words coming out of your mouth, and not know how they got there? That's exactly how I felt. I meant to tell about the stolen packs, but some part of my brain made me ask another one of my geography questions. Weird.

For a minute Mr Santucci just looked down his bifocals at me. Then the opera music started up again, and he seemed to relax a bit.

– You wanna know where am I a from? he asked.

– Yeah, I said.

Behind the counter, way up on the wall, there was this big poster of sausages and cheeses arranged into a map of Italy, which is shaped like a lady's boot. Mr Santucci pointed to a spot down by where the lady's heel would be.

– It's a little village downa here, he said.

He told me the name, too, but I can't remember. Santa something.

– Was it nice? I asked.

– Was it nice? Yeah, it was nice. If you like rocks and earthquakes, it was a really nice. Beautiful scenery.

– Why did you come to Canada?

– Why? You wanna know?

– Yeah.

– Because you can't eatta scenery, that's why. Look, inna Italy, it's the bastards uppa here who got all the money.

He pointed to a sausage up by the top of the poster. He was getting pretty worked up.

– If you from down here (where he was from) and you want money, you gotta leave, he said.

I couldn't really think of anything to say, and anyway, Mr Santucci just seemed to want to get this stuff off his chest. I don't think he expected me to say anything. So I started for the door, but just as I was stepping out, I turned around.

– I saw Giuseppe with an axe in the park, I said.

Mr Santucci must have been still mad about those rich guys in Italy, because he didn't hear me at first.

– You say somethin'? he asked.

– Yeah. I saw Giuseppe in the park by St Paul's. With an axe. It looked like he was trying to chop down a tree.

I don't really know what I expected. I guess I thought Mr Santucci would get mad, and ask for more details. But he stayed calm. He walked out from behind the counter, slowly, right up to me. My eyes were level with a big red stain on his apron.

– You gotta lotta nerve, he said.

He was so quiet I could barely hear him.

– Pardon me? I said.

– I said you gotta lotta nerve. You kids. You come into my store, you hang around buggin' my customers, you steal my stuff, and now you makin' up some crazy story about my son. Giuseppe with a axe. That's the craziest thing I ever heard.

– But ...

– But a nothin'. Get outta my store. And don't show your face inna here again.

He said more, but it was in Italian. I turned around and left.

I walked about half a block before I noticed how much my legs were shaking. To try to calm down, I sat on the curb in front of Bronko Vrbak's house.

It took a minute before I could think straight about what just happened. First, I saw Chris stealing something. But instead of squealing on him, which I'm not even sure why I wanted to do in the first place, I squealed on Giuseppe, when I wasn't even totally sure what he'd done. What made me do that? Was I so mad at myself for not squealing on Chris that I panicked and squealed on Giuseppe, just so it wouldn't be a total loss? I thought about Chris sitting at home with his two stolen packs, and little Giuseppe getting bawled out (even though Mr Santucci said he didn't believe my story) when he's not even really old enough to know what he's doing. I felt like a jerk, and there was nothing I could do about it. If I went back to the store, Mr Santucci would probably come at *me* with an axe.

TEN

It was getting a little late in the lunch hour by now. I couldn't sit
around all day thinking, so I got up and kept walking home. To
try to take my mind off stuff, I concentrated on things around
me. Right at my feet was the gutter by the curb where a bunch of
us have toothpick races in the spring. It's just slightly downhill
from St. Paul's to 92nd street, so if you put a toothpick in the
water that the melting snow makes, it'll run all four blocks until
it goes into the sewer in front of the Pippigs' place. You only have
to pick it up at the crosswalks. There's not really any skill
involved, and it's hard to tell the toothpicks apart, so there's
always a fight about who won, but it's fun.

I cut through Vrbaks' yard into the back alley, and
remembered learning to ride a bike. It happened last summer. Me
and most of my friends were still riding trikes around. When
you're seven or eight, though, you start feeling like a real dork on
a trike. You have to pedal like mad to get anywhere, your knees
keep bumping into the handlebars, and it's almost impossible to
pop a wheelie. So when Bronko Vrbak got a brand new kid's size
bike from George's Cycle on 118th Avenue, it was a really big
deal in the neighbourhood. Everybody crowded around it,
stroking the crowbar and ringing the bell and kicking the tires to
test for air. Finally Bronko got fed up and took off on the bike. I
hung around on his driveway, though, and when Bronko got back
I was the only one still there.

– Mind if I try? I asked.

Bronko looked at me, and looked at the bike. I don't think he
wanted to let me, but he still owed me a favour from the time I
helped him finish his Gulf Coins of the World collection. I gave
him the one from Laos, which is right by Vietnam.

– Do you know how to ride, even? he asked.

– Sure, I said.

That wasn't actually true. But I mean, if you ask to take
somebody's car for a spin, you don't tell them you can't drive, do
you? So I lied a bit.

59

– Well, okay, he said. But only to the end of the alley and back.

So I hopped on, and got a running start down the driveway. I was almost at the end of the alley before I even got my feet on the pedals, so I just kept going, with Bronko yelling 'Hey! Hey!' way behind me. At first I was swerving all over the place, but pretty soon I got control and started tearing around the block. I'll never forget that minute when I first realized I was riding. It was like that part in *Chitty Chitty Bang Bang* when the car first takes off and starts flying. You feel like you can go anywhere. I headed off in the direction of 137th Avenue, and for the first time in my life, I crossed it. I wasn't supposed to, because it's as busy as a freeway, and on the other side all these new neighbourhoods were getting built, so the streets weren't paved and all these gigantic pieces of machinery were lying around. The only finished thing was the sidewalks, so there were these perfect sidewalks with nobody to walk on them, and these half-finished houses that looked more half wrecked, like they'd been bombed. It reminded me of these pictures in *National Geographic* of this town in Italy that got buried in lava from a volcano. When they scraped the lava away the shapes of everything were still there, but there was no life. When I finally got back to Bronko's place, all he said was 'Give it here!' and he grabbed the bike back. He never really talked to me after that.

Riding a bike, even just once like I did, really changes how you think about how far away things are. You start imagining going to places that you'd never think about walking to, like 118th Avenue, where my sister Susan tells me they have these really neat cafés and bars and a record store. You'd think I would have started begging Mum and Dad for a bike, but I didn't. I was happy just thinking of where I could go if I had one. Dad says I might be able to get one next spring.

I snapped out of my daydream when I saw this white streak out of the corner of my eye, coming straight at me. It took a minute to figure out that it was Sam, who'd seen me, or smelled me, from a block away. He runs so fast he has a hard time stopping, so he skidded a few feet past me, then we raced home, down the same part of the alley where a bunch of us used to have imaginary Olympic races. I'd always be Harry Jerome, that Canadian runner who had the world record but always got injured in the big races.

When me and Sam got to the back door, Mum got up from the kitchen table where she was having tea with Elfie Pippig. All the mums in the neighbourhood meet all the others for tea or coffee at different times on different days. I remember when I was too young for school and used to hang around the house more, how amazed I was by how all the mums always knew exactly where all the other mums were. Sara Koveleski from next door would be over for a couple of hours, and the minute she left, Elfie Pippig or Mabel Fitzgerald would show up like magic. Not only that, but they were really serious about their conversations. Once they got going, talking about stuff like diapers and back pains and furniture, you practically needed a nuclear warhead to interrupt them. Mary and me would lie under the kitchen table, yanking on Mum's ankles, nagging her for something or other, and every now and then Mum would just say 'Stop it!' without looking down. All we could do was give up and look at the gum wads and boogers stuck under the table. Sometimes, to get attention, we'd spin around on one spot until we fell over or threw up, but not even that usually worked.

Today, Elfie was leaving just as I got home, so Mum and me were the only two there. All my brothers and sisters were having lunch at their schools.

– Take the long way home? Mum asked.

– What do you mean? I asked.

– Take a look at the time, Mum said. Half past ten after twelve.

That meant twenty to one. *The Flintstones* was already over, and I had to go back in about ten minutes. I must have been walking really slow.

– I was stopping and smelling the roses, I said.

That's something she used to tell me I should do.

– How did they smell? she asked.

– With their noses.

That joke doesn't really work with flowers, but I couldn't resist. Mum chuckled a bit just to be polite. As she handed me my peanut butter and brown sugar sandwich, she kept looking at me funny.

– Are you sure you're okay, Rip? she asked.

That's one of her nicknames for me. Rip was this guy in a book who slept through everything.

– A-okay, I said.

We just sat there for a while, me eating, and Mum humming this old song called 'Istanbul, Not Constantinople'. She knows a million of these weird old things. Some of them are great for learning geography. There's another one that goes 'Tampico, Tampico, on the Gulf of Mexico'. Those old songs kill me.

– Mum? I said a minute later.

– Yaish?

– Is it good to chop down trees?

– That all depends.

– On what?

– Well, on where the tree is, and why it's being chopped. We need trees for wood and paper, after all.

– Could you give me an example of when it's bad?

– I suppose if someone were to cut one down without a licence, or just for fun, that would be bad.

– What if a little kid tried to cut one down in a park?

– That would fall into the bad category, I'd say.

– Oh.

– Neil?

– Yeah?

– Is there any particular point to this line of questioning?

– What do you mean?

– Well, why this sudden concern over the rights and wrongs of tree chopping? Have you been feeling that lumberjack urge lately?

– No. Uh, I'm just working on a list of wrong things, for religion class.

That was partly a lie and partly not. We do have to list sins sometimes for Sister Arlene. It's practice for our first confession or something. But of course that's not why I was asking about the tree. This whole Giuseppe thing was really messing me up. Here I'd already squealed to his dad about it, and I was scared to tell my own mum. Why couldn't I just shut up about it? Weird.

– Well, you've got an original one for your list, she said.

– What? Oh, yeah.

Sometimes I get the feeling Mum knows perfectly well when I'm fibbing. If she thinks it's not too serious, she'll let it go, but she also knows exactly how to find out the truth, like this one time when I was in grade one. I decided one day that I wanted to go home early from school. I asked the teacher if I could go to the bathroom, and I grabbed my coat on the way and just kept going. There was this neat feeling of freedom, walking home alone from school with all the other kids still there and the teacher not knowing where I was, but at the same time there was this funny feeling in the back of my mind. I'd decided everything so fast that I didn't really plan the part about explaining to Mum why I was home at 10:30 in the morning.

When I got in, Mum and Sara were watching Ed Allen's exercise show. All the mums watch him all the time. They never exercise, though. They just sit and watch, smoking or drinking coffee while Ed touches his toes or sticks out his chest. I walked right past Mum and Sara, up the stairs and into my room. A few minutes later, there was a knock on the door.

– Who is it? I asked.

Bright question. Who else would it be? Mum opened the door and sat next to me on the bottom of the bunk-bed. She had to squeeze in.

– Neil? she said.

– Yeah?

– Do you want to tell me why you're here?

There weren't that many lies to tell, so I told the obvious one.

– I got sick.

– Oh? What kind of sick?

– I think I have a fever.

Fevers are weird, because other times I've thought I had a fever, I didn't, and when I have had fevers, I've felt fine. Still, I thought it sounded pretty good.

– In that case, we'd better take your temperature, Mum said.

She came back in a minute with a thermostat and I stuck it under my tongue. I was having a hard time keeping my mouth closed because it was filling with gob, and I was also concentrating on looking sick. Finally, Mum took it out and checked it.

– Hmm, everything normal, she said.

– That's weird, I said.

For a minute, neither of us said anything. I sat staring at Duncan's blacklight poster on the wall, of a guy with a melting face saying 'Stoned Again!' The silence was bugging me, so I said something.

– I threw up too.

– You've just remembered that you threw up too?

– Well, I didn't really throw *up*.

– Oh?

– I mean, I did, but it didn't go on the floor.

– No?

– Yeah. The janitor saw me about to throw up, and he stopped the puke with his mop.

– Really?

– Yeah.

– Neil?

– Yeah?

– If I called your teacher, what would she say?

– She doesn't know. It happened in the hallway.

– All right, if I called and talked to the janitor, what would he say?

– Mr Dimopoulous? His English isn't very good. I don't think you should call him.

It didn't take a genius to figure out I was fibbing my face off. Some mums I know would have called their kid a liar, or grounded him, or whomped him one, but Mum just gave me this sad look, shook her head, and left the room, which made me feel ten times worse. Later, she told me the story of the boy who cried wolf, but by that time I'd already promised myself not to try that kind of thing again.

Compared to that lie, the one today about Giuseppe didn't seem quite so bad, but I was still feeling kind of guilty when it was time to leave for school again. Even Sam could tell something was wrong. Instead of trying to take off after me, which he usually does, he just lay flat on the kitchen floor giving me this weird look. I was turning from the yard into the alley when I heard Mum yelling something.

– What? I yelled back.

– I said, don't forget to come straight home from school today. We've got a lot of work to do.

– Sure, I said.

What she'd said didn't seem like that big a deal. Usually, when

I have to clean the bedroom or rake leaves or something, she or Dad will say there's work to do. It was a bit weird, though, that she said 'a lot'. What was all this work, anyway? I decided it must have been some surprise project, maybe hollowing out some Halloween pumpkins.

I walked up the alley on the way to 93rd Street. Whenever there's a choice, I walk in alleys and not streets. They're just more interesting. Before the back alleys in Glengarry were paved last year, me and Keith used to do geological research. We'd go in the alley with his dad's sledgehammer, pick out some rocks, and smash them in two or three pieces. Then we'd look at the different layers of colour inside, and compare them to the pictures in my brother Howard's high school science book. One day we got really excited when we realized that the colours in one rock looked exactly like a picture of the earth, where it was chopped to show all the layers going down to the core. That got us imagining. What if the rock was really a mini-earth, with living things on it that were too small for us to see? It was a neat idea, until we thought that if it really was a mini-earth, we'd just destroyed it with a hammer. We might have just killed millions of innocent people. That got us thinking that the earth we live on might just be a rock in a back alley on some other planet someplace, and that some kid who lived there might smash us any time, with no warning. It makes you think.

Just before the end of the alley, I passed the Bucyks' back yard. They're the most famous people in Glengarry by far. Bill Bucyk, their dad, is the brother of Johnny Bucyk, of the Boston Bruins, who's one of the leading scorers in NHL history. Sometimes Johnny comes and visits in the summer, and all the kids and some of the adults in the neighbourhood crowd around. It's really weird to see somebody in person who you just saw on TV a little while before, playing with Bobby Orr for the Stanley Cup. You feel like touching him to see if he's real. It's also weird to see Johnny and Bill standing side by side. They look almost exactly the same, yet one's on his way to the Hall of Fame, and the other's just a dad in the neighbourhood, a guy we see taking out the garbage and mowing the lawn and stuff. It's hard to picture Johnny Bucyk taking out the garbage. He probably pays somebody to do that.

65

The Bucyks live right on a corner, so their front yard is small but their back yard is huge. Every year, as soon as it's cold enough, the parents start flooding the yard to make a rink. When they're finished, it's practically as big as a real one. Once or twice every winter there's a game of shinny where everybody can join in, but usually it's just the Bucyk brothers, Terry, Greg and Randy, practising, sometimes for twelve hours a day. Me and Keith used to watch them through a knothole in their fence. They set up this board in front of a net, with a hole in each corner and a painted goalie who looks like Jacques Plante. They drill shots into the holes like it was the easiest thing. Everybody says they'll all be in the NHL some day. It would be neat if Randy made it, because he's the same age as me. We've never really been friends, though, because he's too busy practising, and also because he goes to the Protestant school. It's hard to make friends with guys in different schools.

I turned left, and avoided Santucci's store by walking behind the row of shops that it's in. Not that I was really scared of Mr Santucci, I just hadn't had time to plan my next story to him. Behind the shops is where you always see people from St. Mary and O'Connor smoking. You can tell who's been smoking a long time and who hasn't, because some of them will be blowing fancy smoke rings and letting the cigarette sort of hang from their bottom lip, and other people will be hacking and choking and burning their fingers when they try to light up. One time I walked by and saw Susan smoking. She was only about fourteen then, hanging out with her friend Wanda, who's always the first one to try stuff. Susan saw me and made the 'shh' sign, meaning I wasn't supposed to tell Dad. Smokers don't seem to realize that you can tell they smoke by their smell. Anyway, Dad smokes, so how mad could he get? I don't think I'll ever smoke, because I have a fear of fire. I can never light a match.

Past the stores, it's another block up 132nd to St. Paul's. It's interesting to look at the houses. Almost all of them were built right around 1962. You can tell because every block or so there's a little mark on the sidewalk that tells what year they put it there. Because the houses are the same age as me, I feel kind of related to them. There's pictures of our family when we first moved to Edmonton, standing in front of our new house, and all the front lawns are mud, with boardwalks for sidewalks, and a pig farm where Northgate Mall is now. It's weird to think that was only nine years ago, because already Glengarry looks like it's always been there, with big tall trees and cracks in the sidewalks. About once every two blocks you see a house that looks about fifty years older than all the others. Dad told me they're old farmhouses. The people in them sold their farms so houses could be built on them. You'd think the people in the old places would be rich, but whenever you see them in their yards, they look kind of like Keith's baba, really old people with funny clothes who have huge gardens with scarecrows.

The closer you get to school the more people you see, so as I was walking up 132nd I saw a bunch. There was Wade Two Feathers, who's the only Indian kid I know. He misses school a lot. I also saw Judy, the girl who gets picked on a lot. She must be used to it, though, because it doesn't seem to bug her much. She just stares straight ahead. One time last year, in arithmetic class, a bunch of girls were singing some song about her leotards, but she just ignored them and kept scribbling in her book. Later, I peeked at her book and saw that she wasn't just scribbling. It was full of all these amazing drawings of horses and mountains and princesses and stuff. She'll probably be a famous artist some day. All those other girls will feel like idiots.

A little bit ahead of me, just going into school, I saw Keith and Freddy together. They're not really friends, so I wondered what they were doing. Once, in the basement at my place, Freddy played Keith a bunch of soul songs from a K-Tel record, to try to get Keith into it, but Keith didn't pay much attention. He's not really interested in music. Freddy is, but it's pretty much soul or nothing for him. One time he started bugging me because I was looking at a CHED chart.

– Aw, man, why you waste your time with that stuff? he said.

– Waste my time? I asked.

I didn't know what he meant. Looking at CHED charts is one of my favourite things.

– Yeah, said Freddy. You heard me. I've listened to those turkeys. All they play is rock and roll all day.

– That's not true, I said. They play soul, too. Look, here's Sly, right at number three. 'Hot Fun in the Summertime'. And here's

Diana Ross, and the Temptations, and …

– Hey, they've gotta play *some* soul. Cats would have a riot on their hands if they didn't.

– And what's wrong with rock, anyway? I asked.

– Let me put it to you this way, man, said Freddy. White people are always trying to sound black, am I right?

– I don't know. I don't think Gordon Lightfoot sounds …

– Look, I don't know who this Foot man is, but it's a fact that white singers are always trying to sing like us, play like us. Trying.

– Well, yeah, but …

– Well, yeah, but, can you tell me one brother that ever tried to sound white? One brother that plays that acid rock garbage?

– What about Jimi Hendrix? He's not trying to sound white, but he plays wild guitar solos and stuff.

– Aw, man, that cat is weird. He ain't a fair example.

– But he's black.

– My old man tells me the cat's got Indian blood. Cherokee or something. So maybe that's why he's not funky.

– Not funky? What about 'Foxy Lady'?

– Didn't dig it.

– 'Purple Haze'?

– Did not dig it.

– Have you heard Hendrix, even?

– Look, may the cat rest in peace and all, but he was not James Brown, he was not Sly, he was not Marvin.

– But he was still great.

– Not by my definition.

I could tell I wasn't going to change Freddy's mind about Hendrix, but I thought of something that I figured might hurt his argument a bit.

– Freddy?

– What?

– What about the Beatles?

– What about 'em?

He looked a bit nervous.

– Well, I said, they're white, they play rock, and when I've played their 45s you've really liked them. You were dancing to 'Get Back', and singing along with 'Instant Karma'.

– Hey, man, I thought 'Get Back' was by brothers. So they're good at imitating. Don't prove nothin'. And that other song, I was diggin' the meaning behind the words. The philosophy. Not the music. It's two different things.

– Oh.

Since then I've never really bothered to argue with Freddy about anything. Well, I do, but I never expect to win. You can't. Anyway, seeing him and Keith together made me think of a neat plan. I'd ask both of them if they wanted to come over and watch the game tonight.

ELEVEN

When I got upstairs into the hallway, where my locker is, I saw a big crowd around Tommy Winchester. He was showing his *Man, Myth and Magic* again. This time it was pictures of this tribe in Borneo or someplace, who have this ceremony where the men jump off these high bamboo towers with vines tied to their ankles. Just when they're a few inches from hitting the ground headfirst, the vine stops them, and they bounce back up a bit. They don't just do it for fun, either. It's some religious thing. I tried to imagine jumping off a huge bamboo tower on Sunday mornings at St Paul's church, but I couldn't.

Seeing a bunch of people around Tommy was nothing new. He's just one of those guys. He's either all alone or with a ton of people. When he first moved here, it was the middle of grade three. It's always a big deal when somebody new comes, but Tommy was different for two other reasons. One was how long his hair was. We weren't even sure he was a guy at first. We thought maybe he was a girl with a boy name, like some girls are called Bobby. The other thing was that he was American. Most of us had never met a real American before. The only other ones I ever saw were those hippies in Saranac Lake, and lots of hitchhikers when I've gone on trips with my dad. 'Draft dodgers!' he'd say, but he'd always pick them up and we'd all chat. On his first recess, Tommy was treated like a rock star. We all followed him all over the place, and he did things like showing us American money (it looks fake, like Monopoly money) and telling American jokes ('Why do GWGs look so old? Because they're George Washington's gaunch!').

Tommy got interested in me when he found out I was a music fan. I was walking around the schoolyard one day with a couple of albums. I do that a lot. You always think you're going to impress people, but they usually either don't care or think you're weird. Tommy noticed right away, though, and walked up to me.

– Hey, man, lemme see, he said.

I showed him. They were the Beatles, *Hey Jude*, and

Creedence, *Willy and the Poorboys*. He made the yuk face.

– What's your problem? I asked.

– This is *pop* music, he said.

– What do you mean?

– I mean, man, it's top thirty, bubblegum music.

– The Beatles and Creedence, *bubblegum*?

I couldn't believe my ears. Bubblegum, to me, was stuff like Bobby Sherman and the Partridge Family. Plus, this was not long after Freddy chewed me out for liking stuff that wasn't soul music. I spent half my life buying records and listening to the radio and reading the charts, and guys kept telling me I was wrong. It was starting to cheese me.

– Well, what do you like then? I asked.

– You wouldn't have heard of it, he said.

His accent was really starting to get on my nerves all of a sudden.

– Try me, I said.

– I'll tell you what, man. Meet me next recess and I'll show you. But be prepared to have your mind blown.

– Whatever, I said.

Next recess, that afternoon, he called me over behind the portables and pulled two albums out of a bag. One was by a group called Black Sabbath. I noticed that there were only about five songs on it, about ten minutes each. That was weird. The other was by this guy called Jethro Tull, who played a flute and dressed like an old tramp, except with ballet tights. All his songs were long, too. What I really noticed on both the covers, though, was the hair. I mean, I've seen long hair. I've even got pretty long hair myself. But these people had unbelievably long hair. It covered their eyes and went all the way down past their waists. If Monsieur Houle ever saw hair like this he'd do an instant dump in his drawers. I couldn't even imagine what this music must sound like, and I was even a bit scared to find out. What if they were better than the Beatles and Creedence and Sly?

– I'll have you over some day, man, and play them. So brace yourself, Tommy said.

– Sure, I said.

Later that day, Tommy's dad came to pick him up from school. He was driving a rusty old station wagon that still had California licence plates, and on the back was a bumper sticker that said 'Hell, no, we won't go!' And you won't believe it, but Mr Winchester's hair was as long as Jethro Tull's. Most dads look pretty much the same. Some are a bit balder or have bigger guts, but they all look like, you know, *dads*. Not Mr Winchester.

We all had to stop looking at the Borneo pictures when the buzzer rang for the first afternoon class. On my way in, I saw Victor Nedved talking with his Dad, the janitor, in Czechoslovakian. It must be weird having your dad right there in school, and talking to him in front of everybody. At least they don't have to worry about anybody knowing what they're saying.

Mr Nedved is actually pretty different for a janitor. Most of them are older, like Mr Dimopoulous, and they'll sometimes goof around with the kids in the playground. Once Mr Dimopoulous pretended he was a statue. He stayed in this funny pose, shooting out water between his teeth, and let us climb all over him. Mr Nedved is way more serious, though. You see him writing in a notebook, or staring off someplace. You don't see him doing that much janitor work.

TWELVE

In the classroom, I noticed that everybody was more excited than usual, but at first I couldn't tell why. Then I turned around and saw that we had a substitute teacher. Miss Barker must have been sick. People always like having a sub, usually because we know we can goof off, but with this sub it was different. It was Mr Baldwin. We'd had him a couple of times before, and everybody liked him. What he does is forget about what he's supposed to teach and just talk to us. The only one who doesn't like that is Daniela, who thinks he isn't serious enough. I had an argument with her about it once.

– Mr Baldwin's cool, I said.

– Oh, sure, said Daniela. It's very cool not to teach us anything.

– He teaches us lots of stuff.

– Such as?

– Well, like how to talk and stuff.

– Talk? We can talk at recess! We're here to work. Maybe if he talked less and taught more he'd be a real teacher, and not just a substitute.

I quit arguing. I knew I'd never change her mind, but I was also worried she might be right about the job part. There had to be some reason why Mr Baldwin was a sub. He's young, and most subs are old retired teachers with those funny half glasses like Mr Santucci's.

It was also good to see Mr Baldwin because I didn't get along very well with Miss Barker, the usual enterprise teacher. It's because of something that happened about a month ago. Enterprise is history and stuff, so she was talking about the Indians in North America, and how nobody knows where they came from.

– Yes they do, I said.

– Pardon *me*? she asked.

She's not one of those teachers who likes interruptions.

– They do know where they came from, I said.

By now everybody was looking at me. I don't know if they really cared where Indians came from, but it was weird seeing a student telling the teacher she was wrong.

– Oh? And where might that be? Miss Barker asked.

– From Asia.

– From *Asia*? Whoever told you such a preposterous thing?

– It's true. I'll show you, I said.

Before I really knew what was happening, I was walking up to the front of the room, on my way to the big map of the world. Miss Barker just stood there with her mouth open. A few people were giggling. I stood up on my tiptoes to point up to the top of the map, to the Bering Strait between Russia and Alaska.

– They crossed over here, I said.

– And how did they do that? On a big cruise ship? Miss Barker asked.

More people giggled.

– They didn't need a boat, I said.

– Oh, I see. They swam. Must have been chilly.

Now people were really laughing.

– No, I said. They didn't swim either. Thousands of years ago, the Bering Strait wasn't water. It was land. A land bridge. They walked across. You can tell, because Eskimos look the same as people from China and Mongolia and Korea. You can tell they're all from the same place. And the Indians came from them.

I pointed to all those places on the map, and turned around and looked at the class. It was a different feeling from sitting in your desk, to be looking the other way and see all these faces looking up at you. I'd been in front of the class before, for show and tell or to get bawled out, but this wasn't the same. I didn't even feel nervous for some reason, so I kept talking.

– And they didn't start here, either, I said, pointing to Mongolia.

Miss Barker was just staring at me, so I kept going.

– They started way over here, I said.

I pointed to Lake Tanganyika in Africa.

– A famous archaeologist, Dr Leakey, says that ...

– *Thank* you, Mr McDonald.

It was Miss Barker.

– Pardon me? I said.

– I said thank you, Mr McDonald. What you say is very interesting. Now, if you don't mind, I would like to resume my job. Of teaching.

People were laughing again, but this time I got the feeling they were on my side. It felt neat. It wasn't like I was trying to embarrass Miss Barker or anything, I just thought everybody should know the real story. I got it from *National Geographic*. It's not some big secret. I sat back down.

I didn't notice how mad Miss Barker was until I was back at my desk. She was talking really slow, like people do when they're trying to control their temper, and every now and then she'd glare at me. I decided it would be a good idea not to correct her any more that day, so I didn't, even when she said British Columbia was one of the three prairie provinces. After the class, on my way out, she called me over.

– What was the meaning of that? she asked.

– There wasn't any meaning. I just …

– Don't … you … ever … show me up like that again. Do you hear me?

– But I just thought everybody should know …

– The truth? Is that what you want to say? Mr McDonald, leaving aside for the moment your source, whatever it may be, the issue here is not the truth. The issue is one's place. Your place, as a student, is in your seat. My place, as a teacher, is in front of the class. If these places are reversed, we do not have truth, we have anarchy. Do you understand what I'm saying?

– Yes, Miss Barker.

I didn't completely understand. Anarchy was a new word. But yes was the best answer.

– Then you may go, she said.

I left. I thought she was wigging out a bit much for such a small thing, but you see that sometimes with teachers. They'll put up with kids screaming and goofing off for a month, then one day some little thing will make them go hog wild. Mum says it's because they're under a lot of stress. She knows, because she was a teacher. Before she married Dad, she taught in this little one-room school in Ontario. It was one of those schools where all the different grades and ages were together in the same room. That must be weird, for little kids to be learning with people who are practically adults. I remember when I was in grade one, there was a guy in grade six, John, who was a bit retarded. He repeated grade six a couple of times, so he was already a teenager, and he was starting to grow a beard. I can't even imagine being in the same class as a guy who has to shave, or a girl with a big bra.

Today, as we sat there waiting for enterprise class to start, there was that sort of tingle in the air, like in a movie theatre when the lights go down, or when the national anthem at a hockey game ends. You don't know what's going to happen, but you know it's going to be something fun or at least unusual.

The last time Mr Baldwin taught us, about a month before, he brought his guitar to class. He talked for a while about the blues, which is the music that came before rock music, and pointed to a map of the States to show how the blues started in Mississippi and went up the river to Chicago. Then he took out his guitar and demonstrated all these different kinds of blues. At first, all he did was bang on the guitar and shout, something about picking cotton. Each song after that got a bit more complicated. My favourite one was when he picked up an empty bottle, stuck it on his finger, and slid it up and down the strings. It made me think of snakes, if snakes made sounds. Finally, he started making up blues songs about different people in the class. For example, he looked at Brad Flipchuk's feet, and started singing.

Woke up this morning, couldn't find two white socks
Said I woke up this morning, couldn't find two white socks
Put on a white one and a brown one, now I hope nobody mocks me

Everybody laughed their heads off, even Brad, who'd normally clean your clock if you made fun of him. The best part of all was that it was supposed to be arithmetic class, and we didn't take out our books even once.

Another neat thing Mr Baldwin does is in roll call. Instead of just reading everybody's names, he'll make a little comment, or ask a little question.

– Flipchuk, Brad.

– Present.

– Well-coordinated socks today, Brad. Good to see. Livingstone, Fred.

– Here.

– Give your father my regards, Freddy. He still bowls a mean googly.

– Thanks, Mr Baldwin. I will.

They were talking about cricket. It's this weird sport, a bit like baseball, except the pitcher runs about a mile before he throws the ball, and everybody else just kind of stands around in sissy-looking sweaters. Mr Baldwin knows about it because he lived in India for a couple of years. It's really popular there, and also in Trinidad, where Freddy's dad is from. He was a big cricket star there. Mr Baldwin and Mr Livingstone both play on Saturdays in this little park by Victoria golf course, in the river valley. I've seen them a couple of times, when I've been caddying for Dad.

– McDonald, Neil.

– Present.

– How goes the magnum opus?

I didn't know what the last two words meant, but I knew he was talking about the book I said I wanted to write. The trouble was, I said that before I knew what the story would be, and I still hadn't started it, which was kind of embarrassing. So I fibbed a bit.

– It's going really well, I said.

– Good, good. I'll watch for excerpts.

I looked over and saw Daniela pretending to gag.

– Nedved, Victor.

– Here.

Then Mr Baldwin said something in Czechoslovakian. He must have learned it just for Victor. Victor jumped up from his seat, stuck one fist in the air, and sang a couple of lines from a song. It sounded like an anthem. Nobody else knew what was going on.

– Da Silva, Daniela.

– Present.

Something about the way she said 'present' stopped Mr Baldwin from joking with Daniela. You can usually tell who's worth cracking a joke to and who isn't. Mr Baldwin finished the last few names, then turned around and wrote one big word on the blackboard: DEMOCRACY.

– Here's a word you hear a lot, he said. Some of the people

who use it know what it means, and some don't. Can anybody tell me?

Nobody stuck their hand up right away, so he turned around and underlined the first few letters.

– This, he said, is from the Greek (he wrote some word in these cool Greek letters), which, roughly translated, means 'the people'. And this (he underlined the second part of the word, and wrote another Greek one) means 'rule', or 'govern'. So, putting them together, what have we got?

Everyone shouted out at the same time, either 'People rule!' or 'People government!'. It was wild, because in most classes, only two or three people would bother. Mr Baldwin went bug-eyed and gave a little whistle. We all laughed.

– Recently, he said, in our province, we've seen an example of the practice of democracy. Who can tell me what it was?

Five or six people stuck up their hands, but Daniela was the fastest.

– The provincial election, she said.

– Correct, Miss da Silva. An election in which Alberta's voters, demonstrating all the thought and subtlety of a stampeding herd of cattle, elected a new party by an overwhelming majority. Can anyone tell me the name of our new rulers?

This time I was the fastest.

– The Progressive Conservatives.

– Indeed. The Progressive Conservatives. Two words which, by the way, are entirely opposite in meaning, and make no sense used together. But never mind, this is the party that will lead us to unprecedented prosperity.

It was cool how you could pretty much understand Mr Baldwin, even though he kept using big words. Most teachers try to talk kid talk and put you to sleep. The only thing with Mr Baldwin was, you couldn't always be sure when he was serious and when he was kidding.

– I'd like everyone to be perfectly silent for a minute, he said.

So we all went quiet. The only sound in the room was Carl Wysocki squeaking his Hush Puppies, and even that stopped when Mr Baldwin went and stood on his foot. We all laughed for a minute, and then there was no sound in the room at all. Mr

Baldwin put one hand to his ear, like he was listening to a faraway noise.

– Can you hear it? he asked.

– Hear *what*? asked Daniela.

– The traffic? asked somebody else.

– No, no, said Mr Baldwin.

– The radio? I asked.

You could just barely hear that song 'Joy to the World' by Three Dog Night, coming from a transistor somebody had in front of O'Connor.

– No! No! Not the radio! Not the traffic! You're just not *trying*, Mr Baldwin said.

It was driving us all nuts.

– Do you mean to tell me you really don't hear it? That low, sort of splooshing sound? Well, you'll learn to recognize it, because that's the sound of *oil*. We're sitting on top of an ocean of oil.

We all listened again. Some people said stuff like 'Oh, yeah, I hear it now.'

– Yes, an ocean of oil. There's one problem, though. It's a very thick, sticky ocean. In fact, it's more like glue. And to make it into real oil, the kind we can put into our gas tanks, is going to be very expensive. But the Progressive Conservatives say we can do it, and we believe them. One day, we're told, every man, woman and child in Alberta will be able to retire on our newly found, evenly distributed wealth.

– You mean we'll all be rich? Victor asked.

– Filthy, said Mr Baldwin.

– *Yeah!* shouted Victor. Other people were whistling and going 'Wow!'

– Yes, Mr Baldwin said, and not only will we all be wealthy, but the rest of Canada, far from being envious, will be only too pleased to work as our butlers and chauffeurs.

I tried to picture Uncle Howard driving me to school, or Aunt Pat scrubbing our kitchen floor, but I couldn't. That's when I started to think Mr Baldwin was kidding.

– And those pesky winters of ours? We'll build giant plastic bubbles over Edmonton and Calgary. Mountains? Let's face it, other than two or three for skiing, how many mountains do we really need? We'll level the rest and put up golf courses. If the animals don't like it, well, they can always go to B.C.

By this time, pretty well all of us knew he was joking, but nobody was laughing that hard, because they'd been excited for a minute about getting rich. That's what I mean about Mr Baldwin. He keeps you guessing. But it's the same whenever anybody talks about the future. There's that show on TV, *Here Come the Seventies*, about all the stuff that's going to happen in the next ten years. Our food will just be little pills, machines will make all the music, and we'll all walk around naked. It's hard to believe some of it, especially the naked part. There's no way I'd do that, unless everybody else did. If there was even one guy with clothes on laughing, it would be too embarrassing.

Mr Baldwin stopped talking about democracy and the future for a minute, and said a bit about the history of Alberta. That's what we were supposed to be studying.

– Just this past summer, he said, a new tourist attraction opened in our city.

– Fort Edmonton! a bunch of us yelled.

We all knew because most of us went to the grand opening. It's this big place built to look like a fur-trading fort from two hundred years ago. They gave all the kids free balloons.

– Correct again. And why was the original Fort Edmonton built?

Daniela was the fastest again.

– It was a trading post. Indians came there to trade with settlers and trappers.

– Very good, Daniela. They traded. Now, what exactly was traded, and by whom?

– The Indians and Métis gave fur to the Hudson's Bay Company, Daniela said.

How did she know all this, anyway? She just came from Brazil.

– Yes, and what was given to the Indians? Mr Baldwin asked.

Daniela was stuck. She didn't know. We all tried thinking of things the Indians might have got.

– Clothes? Brad Flipchuk asked.

– Food? Leslie Wilson asked.

– Good guesses, even correct in part, even though the Indians were more than capable of clothing and feeding themselves. But they got something else too, a new product.

Nobody knew what he was talking about.

– I'll give you a clue. I'm not exactly sure what you've been taught about how this part of the country was settled, if anything. You may have some idea that it was like that swill Hollywood serves up, cowboys and Indians, et cetera. The fact is, we would not be here today if the Indians hadn't extended a welcoming hand to the explorers and traders. The natives were not hiding in the bushes waiting to scalp people. They were more like tour guides. This relationship went on for at least two hundred years, more or less to everyone's benefit. Gradually, though, that hard-won trust was abused by people who saw that they could get better deals if the natives were first provided with a certain something. Think about a drink, a golden-coloured drink often served at parties.

– Ginger ale? somebody asked.

– No.

Then I realized.

– Whisky! I shouted.

– Right, said Mr Baldwin. Whisky. Or firewater, as the homemade brand was called. Does anybody know what whisky does?

I took a sip of some once, thinking it was pop, when Dad had some work friends over.

– I do, I said. It gets you drunk really fast.

People giggled. It must have sounded like I drink whisky all the time.

– Yes, really fast, said Mr Baldwin. Now imagine that you've never had whisky. Your parents and grandparents have never had whisky. There is nothing in your body, or in the culture of your people, to defend you against this new drink. Very quickly, though, your body gets to like it, or at least thinks it does. Before you know what's happened, your body is asking for this drink. All the time. You do whatever you can to get more. You are addicted. Addicted to the point where you don't notice other things, like the stealing of your land, and the deliberate spread of disease, until it's too late. That is how the West was won.

We all just sat there. It was hard to know what to say. Some people were fidgeting and squirming, not because they were bored, but because the subject was making everybody kind of nervous. It reminded me of the time we watched a film about Hitler and the Nazis. The room was dark, and we started a spitball war while all these pictures of burning books and concentration camps flashed on the screen. When it was over and the lights came back on, there were little spitballs all over the screen, and Miss Rains, our teacher, gave us a big lecture about how disrespectful we were. The thing was, I knew she was right, but it's kind of like the laughing in church problem. There's something about a really serious subject that just makes you want to shoot spitballs or something. It probably won't be such a big problem once I'm a bit older.

Mr Baldwin must have realized things were getting a bit too serious, because he changed the subject and started talking about TV. The last time he subbed he said it would be a good idea if we wrote a little essay about our favourite TV show, why we watched it and why we liked it. But he wasn't back the next day, so we didn't have a chance to talk about it. He reminded us.

– Seen any good TV lately? he asked.

People started shouting out names of shows, stuff like *H.R. Pufnstuff* and *Rocket Robin Hood*. There's not a whole lot to discuss about shows like that, though. Then somebody said *The Time Tunnel*. Mr Baldwin had never heard of it, so we had to explain it to him. It's about these two guys, scientists I think. Every now and then, for reasons I don't really understand, they step into this long, swirly tunnel and land somewhere in the past. The tunnel doesn't seem to work for the future. Some things about the show are kind of hard to believe. For example, they never land in an ocean, or in a volcano. It's always into a nice soft haystack or something. Also, they never end up anywhere boring or ordinary. They're always in a really exciting time and place in history, right in the middle of the action. So there'll be, like, the French Revolution going on, and these two dorky-looking guys in turtleneck sweaters will stick their noses in. They'll hang around just long enough to make sure history goes the way it's supposed to, then hop back in their tunnel.

– So, let me see if I've got this, said Mr Baldwin. We are where we are today thanks to the retroactive efforts of two scientific American sleuths?

– Yeah! said a bunch of us, even though we weren't sure what he meant.

– Well, said Mr Baldwin, given the state of the world, it's as likely an explanation as any. And come to think of it, the concept does present us with some interesting ethical, not to say logistical, questions vis-à-vis the desirability of time travel. Any comments?

Nobody said anything.

– Uh, let me rephrase that. If you could go back in time, would you?

Just about everybody said stuff like 'Yeah!' and 'Neat.'

– Okay, then. Where, and to what time in history, would you go?

Freddy stuck up his hand, and Mr Baldwin nodded at him.

– I'd go back to Africa, five hundred years ago, said Freddy. I'd find out what life was like for my people before all that slavery and shit.

We all went quiet, because that last word was a definite no-no. Mr Baldwin didn't seem to notice, though. He just smiled at Freddy, and asked if anyone else had ideas. It was like nothing unusual even happened. Tommy Winchester was the next person to stick up his hand.

– I'd go back to Dallas, in 1963, and save JFK.

We all knew who he was talking about. Kennedy was really popular with Sister Arlene because he was the first Catholic president of the States, so she was always mentioning him and his brother, Bobby, who's dead too. Tommy's American, so he's probably heard about them even more.

– Why JFK in particular, Tommy?

– 'Cause he would have kept us out of Nam, and my old man and old lady wouldn't have had to take off.

Not everybody knew what he meant, and hardly anybody was listening anyway, because they were all too busy sticking up their hands trying to give their own answers. After looking at Tommy for a minute, Mr Baldwin let other people answer. Brad Flipchuk said he'd go back to last year's playoffs and help the Leafs beat the Rangers. Daniela said she'd go back and help Florence

Nightingale help wounded soldiers in some war. Victor Nedved wanted to go back and *fight* in some war. After a while, even Leslie Gibson wanted to answer, which was weird, because he hardly ever says anything in class. Mr Baldwin shushed everybody.

– Yes, Leslie? Where would you go?

– I'd go back to prehistoric times.

– Really? How far prehistoric?

– To the Pleistocene era.

People giggled because they thought he'd said plasticine, like Silly Putty or something. I knew what the word was, though. I used to be nuts about dinosaurs. You could collect these plastic dinosaur figures that used to be stuck to the top of pickle bottles. I'd nag Dad to buy them, so we'd always have tons of pickles, way more than we needed, but I got a great dinosaur collection. Sometimes I'd trade with Leslie. The trouble with plastic toys, though, is you always end up chewing them, so I'd end up with, like, a stegosaurus with a long, twisty, chewed-up tail.

– What is it about the period that appeals to you, Leslie? asked Mr Baldwin.

– Just because, said Leslie. There'd be nobody to bother me. I could see what the world was like before people came.

He said the word 'people' like it was some disease.

– Plus, Leslie kept saying, it would be a great chance to study dinosaurs up close. I could learn their habits and live with them, just like they did with the lions in *Born Free*.

It sounded like a really neat idea. The room was really quiet, I think with everybody imagining being back with the dinosaurs. Then somebody said something that wrecked the mood.

– A nice idea, but unfortunately, it makes no sense.

It was Daniela. Mr Baldwin glared at her, and we all turned around to look as she kept talking.

– Dinosaurs died out millions of years before the first people appeared. Atmospheric conditions in the dinosaur era would have been insufficient to sustain human life.

Leslie looked crushed, the poor guy. Mr Baldwin didn't look too happy, either. Even the other students, who never talk to Leslie, seemed to feel bad for him. But Daniela didn't notice. She kept going.

– What's more, even if you could survive physically, how could you possibly function, isolated from other human ...

– That's not the *point!*, somebody shouted out.

It was a voice we'd never heard before, at least not that loud. It took us all a minute to figure out who it was. When we did, we were pretty shocked. It was Carl Wysocki. He was looking right at Daniela, with his eyes all magnified by these thick glasses he wears. He looked like some really mad insect.

– What did you say, Carl? Mr Baldwin asked.

We all knew what he'd said, it was so loud. I think Mr Baldwin just felt like hearing it again. He was smiling as Carl went on, with his Hush Puppies squeaking.

– I *said*, that's not the *point!* So what if it couldn't really *happen*? We're talking about *imagining*! Leslie likes dinosaurs ...

– And penguins! somebody shouted, but Carl ignored it.

– He's interested in dinosaurs. So what's wrong with him imagining living with them? So what if he couldn't really *do* it? That's not the *point!*

By this time Carl's face was all red, and he was squeaking his shoes so loud you could barely hear him. Leslie was all red, too, but also smiling, when a minute before he looked like he'd cry. Mr Baldwin looked at Carl like a proud father. And you should have seen Daniela. She was all white and shaky, shuffling her papers a mile a minute.

– Thank you, Carl, said Mr Baldwin. And thank you too, Miss da Silva, Mr Wilson, and everyone else who has spoken. What we're seeing today is an example of *this* in action.

He pointed back at the word 'Democracy' that was still on the blackboard.

I kept looking over at Daniela. She was still shaking and shuffling and looking like a ghost. Her black hair looked even blacker next to her white face. I actually felt sorry for her. I must have stopped listening for a minute, because when I looked back up, Mr Baldwin was looking right at me, like he was waiting for an answer or something.

– Pardon me? I said.

– I said, what about you, Mr McDonald? You've been uncommonly quiet.

He was right. It was so interesting listening to the answers and arguments and stuff that I forgot to say anything. I hadn't even thought about what my answer would be, so I had to think fast. The trouble was, there's so many great times in history that I'd like to go to that it was hard to decide. I mean, I'd love to go back and sail with Columbus, or play hockey with Rocket Richard, or see the Beatles before they were famous, or go on Captain Scott's Antarctic expedition. There's tons of things. I couldn't pick one, so I just said the first thing that came into my head.

– I'd go back about an hour, I said.

– Oh? And do what?, asked Mr Baldwin.

– Well, it's not really what I'd *do*. It's what I wouldn't do. I mean, I'd go back and stop before I did something.

– Do you want to tell us what you'd do, or wouldn't do, or would have done, or something?

A few people giggled. I was wishing I'd said something else, like the Rocket Richard thing, but it was too late to back out.

– I wouldn't have squealed on somebody, I said.

Mr Baldwin's eyebrows shot up, and everybody else was looking at me like I was a giant turd or something. Mr Baldwin didn't say anything, so I had to keep going.

– I mean, I didn't really squeal. Well, I did, but the thing I squealed about I wasn't really sure about. It probably wasn't even bad.

– And what was it, or can you say? asked Mr Baldwin.

– Umm, well, no, actually I can't.

– Why not?

– That would be squealing.

– Of course. Against the Napoleonic Code.

– Yeah.

Whatever that meant.

I was feeling pretty lousy. People gave all these cool answers, and here I was saying all this stupid stuff, like going to confession but not even telling what you did. I even messed up the little bit I did say, because I didn't mention the part about not squealing on the guy I wanted to squeal on. I thought about trying to set the story straight, but people looked like they were getting bored, so I didn't. I think Mr Baldwin could tell I was stuck, because he changed the subject. I was glad.

– Thank you, Neil, he said. That was, if nothing else, different.

Well, it's certainly a fascinating question. In fact, the whole idea of time travel, and even the nature of time itself, has challenged many a philosopher. There are even those who've said that there is no past, present or future, that these are just concepts imposed by man, with his limited perception.

Now, usually it's fun trying to follow what Mr Baldwin says, but this time he was really losing us. He seemed to realize it, because he started talking a bit simpler.

– When I was in India, I heard a talk by a great man. Some even call him a holy man, although he has nothing to do with any organized religion. His message, which greatly inspired me, boiled down to this: live now. Don't worry about the past or the future. Get the most out of now, and the rest will take care of itself. And right now, it's 1:45. Gotta go.

That's the kind of thing that happens when Mr Baldwin subs. Everybody gets into it, and you can go from talking about some dumb TV show to something really serious. Usually he goes a bit too far, but that's part of the fun. You don't know what's going to happen. Plus, time flies. The class is over before you know it, not like other classes that feel ten times longer than they really are. It's weird, that stuff you like feels shorter than stuff you don't like. It's not really fair.

THIRTEEN

When Mrs Horn came in the door to take us to the art room, it took us all about one second to hop up and get ready to file over. She didn't even get a chance to say 'Hello, class'. People go nuts about art class. You can do stuff you want, and you don't have to worry about hard questions from the teacher, or people laughing at you.

The art room is really wild. It has no windows, but you don't really miss them because the walls are all covered with art by all six grades. It's neat to walk around and look at it. You can see how the way people draw and paint changes the older they get. Stuff by grade ones is mostly, like, stick people with smiley faces. Lots of times you'll see sort of labels, too. Next to one smiley face there'll be the word 'me', or 'Mom', with an arrow pointing to the face. Usually there's a dog or cat or some animal somewhere in the picture, and almost always there's a sun up in one of the top corners, sending shiny rays down on everything. Sometimes you'll see a sun and a moon in the same picture. One weird thing I've noticed is that little kids practically never draw pictures that are inside. There's always a sky.

The older a kid gets, into grade two and three, the more real the pictures start to look. People have bodies instead of just sticks. They're not always labelled. There's not always a sun, and people are inside sometimes. Boys start to draw stuff like sports guys and cars, and girls start doing horses and weddings. People still do this thing where they'll tell their address, starting with 'The Universe' on top and working their way down to Edmonton, their street, their house, and finally their name. Sometimes it's the other way around. Brad Flipchuk used to just sign his stuff 'Me' until the teacher told him that wasn't enough.

Now, in grade four, the main difference is that people fill the whole sheet. Before, there'd be people or whatever crammed down at the bottom, and the sun and maybe some seagulls at the top, with a whole bunch of empty space in between. People aren't so shy about using their pencils and paint now. They go crazy.

88

Victor Nedved does this cool thing where he'll shade in the whole sheet black and then make a picture by erasing some parts of it. It's great to watch. Carl Wysocki will draw, like, the Empire State Building floor by floor, with a little face in every single window. Also, we're learning to draw things other ways than just flat or from the side. It's called perspective. We're figuring it out without the teacher telling us.

Mrs Horn doesn't tell us much. She's not really an art teacher. She used to teach science in Junior High, but one day she freaked out and started throwing test tubes around. They said it was a nervous breakdown. She got a long holiday and when she got back they made her an elementary art teacher. It's a lot more relaxing for her. All she has to do is make sure we don't throw paint on each other or have eraser wars. She'll give a little assignment at the start of the class, something like 'Draw what you feel' or 'Paint your favourite person', then just stroll around the room, looking over our shoulders, saying things like 'That's beautiful' and 'You're very talented'. It's a good way for a teacher to be.

We got our big sheets of construction paper from Mrs Horn and sat around the big round tables. All the paints and pencils and pastels are in the middle of the table. Today there wasn't really an assignment. Mrs Horn doesn't always remember. So we just kept doing what we were doing, or started new pictures. I'd been working for a while on a big picture of Roberto Clemente. I call it a good luck picture, because I started it before the Pirates won the East, and now they were in the World Series. I didn't want to finish it before the Series was over, because I was afraid that would make their luck run out, so I was going slow on purpose, adding more and more details to the background. It was fun.

Actually, I like art way more since I figured out that pictures don't have to look real. Last year, for a project, I tried to draw a picture of the Beatles, the one from the middle of *Sgt. Pepper*, where they're smiling with moustaches. But no matter how hard I tried, I couldn't get it to look right. Even just a tiny mistake would make it look stupid. Ringo would be cross-eyed, or John would be buck-toothed. I took the picture home to work on it more, but Dad or one of my brothers would see it and laugh.

'Look! It's the Geek Beatles!' Duncan said. I got so frustrated I was crying. Tears were falling onto the paper as I drew, making the lead smudge. Then one day, in class, I looked over at Freddy. He was drawing away, a mile a minute, concentrating so hard that his tongue was hanging out, and nothing he drew looked real. It was all weird and cartoony, but he was having fun and the pictures were great. I looked around more, and other people were doing the same thing. Then I thought about this book about art from Spain that I got from the Bookmobile once. These two guys, Picasso and Miro (I wrote down their names), did paintings of people with their faces all twisted, and wormy little shapes floating around. It was stuff any kid could draw. I also thought about Dr. Seuss. He's an artist. So ever since, I don't worry. I finished the Beatles picture and it looked more like they do in *Yellow Submarine*. I still have it.

After a few minutes I stopped drawing and wandered around the room. We were allowed to do that. I looked over Freddy's shoulder.

– What's that? I asked him.

– You mean, *who's* this? he said.

– Yeah. Sorry. Who's that?

The way Freddy paints it's hard sometimes to tell. What he usually does is draw a picture of one of his heroes, somebody like Sly Stone or Clyde Frazier or Muhammad Ali. He'll put a little face at the bottom, and the rest of the sheet will be filled with a giant afro. Inside the afro will be pictures of stuff from that person's life, but drawn really weirdly. You know how when you rub your eyes, you see these psychedelic swirly shapes, and tons of dots? Freddy rubs his eyes, then opens them and draws down what he saw before he forgets. Then, between all the dots and swirls, he'll put the ordinary stuff. I didn't recognize who he was drawing today because there was no giant afro. Then I realized it was somebody white, playing cricket, I guessed.

– It's a cat called Fred Titmuss, Freddy said.

– Fred *who?*

– Titmuss. Wild name, I know. He was a heavy cricket cat. I'm doing this for my old man. He played against him once. England versus West Indies, Port of Spain. Big test match.

– Wow.

– Yeah. You know, I wouldn't be surprised if I was named after this cat. I never thought of that before.

– Freddy Titmuss Livingstone?

– Yeah. Sounds good.

We laughed about that. I thought if I ever had a son, I'd name him Roberto Clemente McDonald. Then I remembered something I wanted to ask Freddy.

– Hey, Freddy?

– Yeah?

– You want to come to my place tonight, and watch the Series game?

– You mean baseball?

– Yeah.

– Aw, man, you know how I feel about baseball. Slow as a snail, and not enough brothers.

He meant black guys.

– But there's lots of brothers on both teams, I said. Frank Robinson, Willie Stargell, Dock Ellis. Tons.

I wasn't sure if Spanish players like Clemente and Cuellar counted as brothers.

– Hey, don't get me wrong, Freddy said. I appreciate the invite. Let me get back to you, okay?

– Sure.

I kept walking around. It's amazing how quiet it gets in art. All I could hear was squeaking pencils and erasers, and slopping brushes. Somebody farted, and only a couple of people laughed. I saw Mrs Horn over by Maria Fadi, this girl with no friends.

– What's that, Maria? Mrs Horn asked.

– The grim reaper, Maria said.

It was this skinny guy with a hood, holding a farm tool like the one my Uncle Howard uses to cut long grass.

– That's beautiful, Mrs Horn said. You're very talented.

– Thanks, said Maria.

A minute later, without meaning to, I ended up right next to Daniela. I'd seen her picture before. It was of all these churches and houses on a hilly street in a Brazilian city, with the ocean in the background. I have to admit it was pretty good. I decided to try something.

– Hey, Daniela, I said.

She pretended not to hear. I think she was still mad about the dodgeball thing in gym.

– Is that in Bahia? I asked.

Her pastel stopped exactly where it was. For a minute she didn't move. Then she turned to me.

– What did you say? she asked.

– I asked if that's in Bahia, I said. That's where it looks like.

She looked pretty shocked. It took her a while to say anything. When she did, it was almost a whisper. I could barely hear.

– How did you know that?, she asked.

– From how hilly it is. And the ocean. Plus, the people look African, and the churches are those old Portuguese kind.

I knew all that from *National Geographic*, and from a show I saw about Brazilian soccer. It was all part of my plan to learn more about Brazil.

– You're right, she said. It's a street in Salvador. My parents used to take me there every Easter. Our nanny in Sao Paulo, Cesaria, was born there. When we left for Canada, she went back.

I realized that for the first time since I met her, Daniela wasn't talking in her big-shot voice. She sounded almost friendly, or at least not all worked up. It would have been neat to keep talking to her like that, but when I went to say more, I could tell by the look on her face that she wouldn't hear. She was just staring into space. Then she seemed to snap out of it, and she bent down to keep drawing, with her face about an inch from the paper. I left her alone.

It's funny, asking people about where they're from, because nobody ever asks me. It must be because I'm not from anywhere different, like Czechoslovakia or Brazil or Trinidad or Ukraine. My family has been in Canada forever. In the graveyard where Mum's grandparents are buried there's a great big tombstone for Simon Fraser. He's got a river and a university named after him. That's how long we've been around. Other people talk about their parents escaping their country in the middle of the night, or learning English by watching *The Friendly Giant*. Stories I could tell about my parents are pretty neat, but they just don't seem as exciting. Like, my dad was born in a silver mining town in Northern Ontario that's not even there any more. It's a ghost town. And Mum's first job after she left the farm was at the

National Mint in Ottawa. If you ever see a penny from 1949 to 1951, chances are my mum touched it. She used to sort them into little piles.

That's the kind of thing I thought about when I went back to my picture and filled in some more clouds in the sky and people in the crowd. The picture was getting too crammed to put much more in. I also couldn't stop thinking of how different Daniela's voice was for just that minute when she was talking about Brazil. I guess people didn't ask her about it very much. I think there should be a class in school where people talk about stuff like that, or just whatever they feel like talking about. But you never get the chance to. Finally, the buzzer rang. Mrs Horn let out this little yelp, told us to put away our stuff, and dismissed us.

FOURTEEN

As soon as we started filing out of the art room you could hear
this sort of screaming from downstairs. That's where the first
three grades are. When it's recess time, and especially hometime,
they go completely wild. They tear out so fast that if you get in
their way you're in trouble. Even though they're so tiny, there's
enough of them to crush you. Upstairs, the top three grades are a
bit more mature. We don't scream, but we're still glad to get out.
We're supposed to go down single file, but that never lasts long.
One person will take off, and the whole line falls apart. I went
out through the courtyard door. To get to the football field I had
to step around these long lines of grade one boys marching and
shouting 'We hate girls!' and girls shouting 'We hate boys!' It was
embarrassing to think I used to do that.

When I got to the field for touch football, a bunch of guys were
already there. Most of the grade four boys who like sports play,
and some grade threes who think they're tough. This is the first
year we've played on the big field between the school and the
church. Other years it was in the playground on the other side,
where the goalposts are kid-sized. It was kind of scary to get to
the big field and see how huge everything was. All of a sudden
soccer goalies had ten times more net to cover, and you had to
kick way higher to get a field goal in football. We still weren't
really used to it. It's so long from one goal line to the other that
by the time you run half the way you're ready to puke.
Sometimes the ball carrier will just stop to rest, and miss scoring
a touchdown.

The two guys who usually take charge of touch football are
Brad Flipchuk and Mario Zoldan, this big guy in another class.
There's not really enough time in recess to pick teams, so Brad
and Mario will just go around to different people going 'Mine …
mine … mine' until there's nobody left. We end up with about
twenty players on each team, and everybody plays at the same
time.

It's kind of stupid how we play. It's touch, so you can't tackle,

94

but we still line up like they do in ordinary football. The offensive linemen, instead of trying to block, just run down the field as fast as they can, hoping to get a pass before somebody on defence touches the quarterback. Even though every play is exactly the same, we still have to huddle and plan them with fancy football language. Today I was on Brad's team.

– Okay, men, gather round, Brad said.

We huddled like you're supposed to, with our arms around each other's shoulders. Some of the shorter guys had trouble reaching. I was glad Chris Ditka wasn't on my team. I would have had to hug him.

– Here's the play, said Brad. Nedved, you snap. McDonald, Smith, Livingstone run post patterns. I'll fake a bomb, go right on a sneak, then go deep.

– Hike! we all yelled.

We had no idea what Brad was talking about.

We walked up to the invisible line of scrimmage, bent over like we were sitting on invisible toilets, and waited for Brad to take the snap from Victor.

– Seventy-five, forty-two blue, set … hut! Brad yelled.

We all took off, except for a couple of guys who stayed back pretending to block. Me and Freddy and about ten other guys were running around in curly lines about twenty yards downfield. We were trying to run post patterns. It was hard to keep from bumping into each other, and to remember who was on your team and who wasn't.

– Open, open! we all kept screaming.

Brad was busy hopping around trying to get away from guys half his size. He looked like King Kong swatting at airplanes. It was pretty funny.

It was right about that time that I started to get this weird feeling. It's happened once or twice before. Everything started to look like it was in slow motion, and I could hear and see everything around me like I had supernatural powers. A robin was chirping on top of the schoolyard fence, there was a long trail of jet smoke way up in the sky with the jet in front looking like a tiny white insect, faces of kids way over by the school entrance looked like they were right up close. I could see Carl Wysocki drawing something with chalk on the courtyard, and Judy pulling up her leotards and Daniela reading a book and Mr Nedved picking up some litter with his pointed stick. The sound of crunching leaves was loud under my feet. All the colours looked twice as bright as normal.

At the same time all this was going on, my head was still right in the game. It was like I knew what was going to happen a split second before anybody else did. Brad got away from a couple of defenders, twirled around like a ballerina, and threw the ball as hard and high as he could. I could see it rising and rising, past the church steeple and the telephone wires and in front of the jet smoke. Somehow I knew where it would come down, and I ran to that spot. Two guys on the other team bumped into each other and wiped out. I was all alone. As the ball came down, the Canadian ball that's fatter than American balls, I could actually read the CFL letters by the stitching. I stuck out my hands over my shoulder, and the ball landed in them soft as a pillow right at the same second I crossed the goal line.

Just as fast as it started, the slow motion feeling went away. I stopped hearing different sounds and just heard one big sound. Things went back to their normal speed. It was like coming up from under water. The whole supernatural thing must have only lasted a few seconds, but it felt like a whole day. I thought how amazing it would be if things were like that all the time. But maybe it's better that it hardly ever happens. It's cooler that way.

I saw my teammates running up to congratulate me, and the guys on the other team just standing around with their mouths open. In a minute people were slapping my back and messing my hair, saying 'Way to go!' and 'Great play!' Even Brad, who I don't think threw to me on purpose, and who's never thrown to me before, was acting like we'd just won the Grey Cup. I tossed the ball back to him, but when everybody started running back to midfield for the kickoff, something stopped me. I just stood there. Thinking about it now, I'm still not sure why. I think maybe there was some little voice saying it would never be any better than this. It was the first touchdown I ever scored, and even if I scored a hundred more, none of them would feel this good. So why not stop now? It's like Sandy Koufax, the Dodgers pitcher who broadcasts Expos games now. Dad said he retired when he was still the best because he was too proud not to be.

I know it's not exactly the same, a kid leaving a recess touch football game and a great pitcher retiring, but the idea is. I remember how sad it was last year, when I watched the Leafs beat the Red Wings 13–0 on TV. Gordie Howe and Alex Delvecchio and Frank Mahovlich, these great players who've been around forever, all of a sudden looked like old men. Toronto guys were skating around them like they were practice pylons. It felt like watching a bunch of kids making fun of your grandfather or something. I wished the ref would just stop it, like they do in boxing when one guy's getting his clock cleaned. I was watching with Dad.

– Dad, this isn't fair, I said.

– It's only a game, Dad said.

– But why does Toronto have to rub it in like that?

– They're only scoring because Detroit's letting them. There's nothing wrong with that.

– But they're making them look stupid!

– Sometimes that's just the way it is.

Toronto scored to make it 9–0, or 10–0, I forget.

– Damnation! Dad yelled.

All of a sudden, he wasn't so calm about it.

– In the old days, Dad said, Gordie Howe wouldn't have put up with this kind of thing. He'd get someone along the boards, wait until the ref wasn't looking, and POW!

He held up his elbow, pretending to be Howe knocking some guy's block off. I cheered like it was real. That got us both feeling better. We pretty much ignored the rest of the game while Dad told stories about when he was younger, watching the Bentley brothers and Ted Lindsay, and Jean Beliveau 'in the old Quebec Seniors League'. He mentions that league all the time. It used to make me picture a bunch of really old French guys skating around, but it was really guys who were still too young to play for the Canadiens.

It's funny, but I sort of think of Dad and Gordie Howe as the same person. They're exactly the same age, they both come from small towns, they even have the same haircut. Maybe that's why I didn't like to see Detroit getting creamed. It makes Dad look old. He isn't, though. He's forty-four. That's old for a hockey player, but still young for a regular guy. Now that Gordie Howe's retired, about a month ago, he can be young again, too.

It's weird how your brain can work like that, mixing up two people until they seem the same, or the way a colour or a smell makes you think of the same thing every time. It happens even more when you're younger and not really sure what's going on. I remember when I was about four or five, and that whole Beatles-Jesus thing happened. John Lennon said the Beatles were getting more popular than Jesus, and people who liked Jesus got pretty mad. I was so young, though, that I got them mixed up. I mean, I sort of knew that the Beatles sang songs on the radio, and that Jesus was the guy in the picture, with the cuts on his forehead and his heart showing through, but people were saying the words 'Beatles' and 'Jesus' together so much that they were the same to me. It didn't help that the Beatles and Jesus were the only men I'd ever seen with long hair. George and Jesus looked like twins. Even now, when I'm in church, and Jesus is mentioned or I see a picture, right away I think of the Beatles. When they split up last year, I couldn't understand why the priest at St Paul's didn't say anything about it. It happened right around Easter time, too.

Anyway, there I was, standing in the end zone, still tingling from the touchdown, watching everybody else start to play again. I looked down at my hands, where I'd caught the ball, like I couldn't believe what they'd just done. I must have stood there for a while, because the next thing I knew the buzzer was ringing to go back inside. I didn't want to. I wished I could have just kept standing there, but that would have been stupid, when you think about it.

Turning to go in, I felt a finger tapping on my shoulder. I turned around and it was Keith. He's one of the guys who doesn't bother playing touch football, even though he's a football fan. I think the reason is because he's a bit chubby. He could probably be a good player, but he's afraid of being called names, or maybe afraid he'll try to beat up the guys who call him names.

– Nice touchdown, he said.

– Thanks, I said.

– Hey, I've got to tell you something.

– Yeah?

I thought it might be something about the game tonight, or some new joke. Keith's always got lots, at least he used to.

– Somebody wants to see you, he said.

He said it in a friendly way.

– Oh yeah? Who? I asked.

– Tony Santucci. He said, 'I wanna talk to your friend, the guy with the hair.'

– Oh, jeez. Oh, man.

I must have looked pretty bad, because Keith got this worried look on his face.

– Hey, what's wrong with you? he asked.

– Oh, man. Tony Santucci. That's Giuseppe's big brother. Oh, jeez.

– I know he's Giuseppe's big brother, Keith said. So what?

I could feel myself going shaky all over.

– Oh, man. Remember at lunch, when I said I saw Giuseppe with an axe in the park?

– Yeah, so?

– Well, I told Mr Santucci that, too. In the grocery store, after you left.

– You *squealed?*

– Yeah. I mean, no. It wasn't really squealing.

– What do you mean?

– I mean, I didn't mean to squeal on Giuseppe. I meant to squeal on Chris.

– For stealing the packs?

– Yeah.

– So why didn't you?

– I don't know. It just happened. Hasn't that ever happened to you?

– Hasn't what happened?

– When you want to say one thing, but you get all nervous and say something else?

– No. But I've never tried to squeal on anybody.

– Great. Oh, man.

– Anyway, it's no big deal. I don't know why you're getting your snot in a knot.

– What are you talking about? Why else would Tony want to see me, except to beat me up for squealing on his brother?

– I don't know. But he was all friendly when he asked. It sounded maybe like he wanted to play road hockey or something.

I've played road hockey with Tony and some of his friends, these even bigger guys who live in Little Italy. A couple of times, when they've needed one more player, they've grabbed me and stuck me in net. I'd stand there getting drilled with the sponge puck while these guys ran around shouting in Italian.

– He wouldn't *ask* me about that, I said. Anyway, it's just too much of a coincidence, that he'd want to see me today. I'm a goner.

– I don't think so, said Keith. Tony's way too big.

– What do you mean?

– I mean, a guy that big wouldn't beat up on somebody that much smaller than him. You just don't do that. Of course, you just don't squeal, either.

– Oh, great. Thanks for your help, pal.

– Hey, I was just kidding. I really don't think Tony will beat you up. Maybe just scare you a bit.

– Easy for you to say. Anyway, we're late.

– Yeah, I guess, Keith said. So, are we watching the game tonight or what?

– You mean you want to? You didn't sound so interested before.

– I was just thinking about other stuff. Of course I want to. Your place at six?

– Yeah. If I'm still alive.

– Great. See you then.

– Sure.

We went in, splitting up at the top of the staircase. I kept wondering what it would be like to get beat up. It's never really happened to me. There was this one kid a couple of years ago, Leonard, who used to hide in the alley behind 132nd and attack kids as they went by. One day he jumped me from behind and did that *Stampede Wrestling* move where you pull a guy's nose up and pull his jaw down. The whole thing was over in a minute. It didn't seem to hurt that much, but it must have been pretty bad because when I saw my reflection in a car window, there was blood all over my face. I washed it off in the can at the Gulf station, otherwise Mum would have freaked out. It's weird that it didn't hurt more. I've heard stories about how boxers, or soldiers in a battle, can get so worked up that they don't feel pain. Maybe that's what happened to me. Still, I don't really count that time as getting beat up. Leonard got sent to a boys' school a little while after that.

FIFTEEN

There wasn't a whole lot of time to think about getting beat up by big Italian guys, because arithmetic class was about to start. Sister Arlene was the teacher. You always get your home room teacher for the first and last class of the day. She was actually a pretty good teacher to have right at that time, because she took my mind off things. You have to concentrate so hard on not getting bawled out or embarrassed that you don't have time to worry about other stuff, like big Italian guys breaking your arms.

Arithmetic is one subject I really don't like. I do okay in it, but I can't get excited about it. It's hard to have discussions and arguments like you might in enterprise class or reading. What can you say about a bunch of numbers? Are you going to fight over an answer, say 'No! I don't agree that five times four is twenty, I say it's nineteen!' In arithmetic, you're either right or you're wrong. Some people, like Daniela, really like that. Of course, she would. She's right all the time. Ask somebody who's wrong all the time, like Victor, and he might tell you different. For me, it's just boring. I look at a page in the textbook, and in a minute the numbers start dancing around, like when I'm reading in bed just before I fall asleep.

Most arithmetic classes, Sister will introduce a new idea, or add a couple of rows to the multiplication table, and then give us exercises for practice. Today was different, though. She gave us this huge homework assignment last week that nobody could finish. Parents were complaining that their kids, who'd never had homework before, were all of a sudden getting hours and hours of it, and crying and losing sleep. So today we got class time to finish the homework. That was good because it meant we didn't have to worry about getting asked questions, but bad because it was hard to concentrate. We had to just sit there working on the problems without a peep.

All this stuff was helping me keep my mind off Tony Santucci, but I wasn't getting much arithmetic done. I'd focus my eyes on the page long enough to do a couple of questions, but then I'd lose it again. Sister was walking around the room, making sure people weren't cheating, and pointing out wrong answers so people could try again. I looked over at Daniela and she'd done about forty questions out of fifty. I was only on number fifteen. Even Victor and Brad were way ahead of me, so I figured I'd better catch up before Sister got around to me. Otherwise it would look pretty suspicious. So I started going faster, just making up wrong answers if I didn't know the right one.

It was right about then that I noticed a poking feeling up by the top of one leg. There was something in my pocket. I stuck my hand in to feel what it was, and I couldn't believe it. It was a pack of baseball cards, the one I'd bought almost three hours ago at Santucci's. It felt like a year ago. That showed what a weird day I was having, because normally I tear open a pack the minute I buy it. To forget for three hours was really bizarre.

I pulled the pack out of my pocket, slowly so the wrapper wouldn't make a loud crinkly sound. It must have made a bit of noise, though, because Daniela stopped writing for a second and looked over and rolled her eyes. I had to be careful to keep the hand with the pack in it under the desk, and to keep writing with the other hand. Once I knew I had the cards, though, it was impossible to keep doing multiplication questions. I was writing down numbers, but they might as well have been doodles. All I could think about was what players were in the pack. I looked down at it in my hand. It was curved a bit from being in my pocket for so long, but it wasn't bent. That was good.

I looked up to see what Sister was doing. She was still walking around the room, about three rows over, making her way across. What could I do? I couldn't go on pretending to do questions, because by now the pencil was shaking so hard in my hand I thought I'd drop it. But I couldn't put the pack back in my pocket either. It's hard to explain why. I just couldn't. Just when I thought I'd start crying or screaming with suspense, Sister must have got tired, because she turned around and walked back to her desk. Here was my chance.

I took a minute to take a few deep breaths and stop shaking. This wasn't going to be easy. Normally you need two hands to open a pack, so I had to take a chance and put the pencil down, but I must have still been pretty shaky, because the pencil missed the little slot and rolled down the desk onto the floor. In such a quiet room, it made a sound like pots and pans crashing. Daniela looked over again. I leaned over to pick it up, and as I was straightening up, I saw something that almost made me pee myself. Sister was looking straight at me. She had that 'I know exactly what you're up to' look. That's pretty much how she always looks, but it still made me freeze. For a second we just stared at each other, but then she looked back down at what she was doing. I wiped the sweat off my forehead and put the pencil down again, this time in the slot.

Opening the pack took some planning. Tearing the little glued part is really loud, so I thought I'd wait for some other noise that would cover it, and do it really fast. It took a minute, but Carl Wysocki started squeaking his shoes, and I ripped the pack open. Then I had to unfold the wrapper. That's pretty loud, too, but in a while a car outside on 132nd honked its horn, and I managed okay. I flattened the wrapper with the back of my hand, and stuck it between the pages of one of my scribblers. The unwrapping was done. Now I could put my writing hand back on top of the desk, because I've taught myself the trick of the trick of flipping through cards with one hand. It was coming in handy now.

I looked down. There were the cards, with the gumstick on top. The gum you get in baseball cards is the worst in the world. It tastes like pink cardboard with a bit of icing sugar sprinkled on. One time me and Keith did an experiment. We left an unwrapped gumstick on a window sill in the basement of my house for two weeks, then snapped it in two and each chewed a half. It tasted exactly like it always does. I wasn't sure what to do with the stick today, so I ducked my head down for a second and stuck it in my mouth. I was afraid chewing it would make too much noise, so I stuck it with my tongue to the top of my mouth, like you do with a communion wafer. You're not supposed to chew those. They're the body of Christ.

I looked at the top card. Gates Brown, Tigers. Got him already. Most doubles are only good for trading, but some, of really great or unusual players, are worth keeping because they could be really valuable someday. I'd keep the Gates Brown, I thought, because he holds the all-time record for pinch hits.

I flipped to the next card: 1971 Rookie Stars, Greg Luzinski and Leron Lee. Got it already, too, but I'll keep it because you never know which rookies will end up all-stars, or even Hall of Famers. If you had Willie Mays's rookie card now, you could buy a house with it.

Next card. Jose 'Coco' Laboy, Expos. Great. That makes thirty-one of him. The people at the card company must get together every winter and decide which player will have ten times more cards than any other, just to drive people nuts. Plus, it's got to be a player nobody cares about in the first place. Maybe some day I'll cover a whole wall in my room with them. Coco Laboy wallpaper.

Seven more cards to go, and still no new ones. Flip. Yeah! All right!! Cesar Gutierrez, Tigers. He's a big deal for two reasons. One, I didn't have him before. Two, last year he went 7-for-7 in one game. That's a major league record, so he's a collector's item. Already, this was a good pack. This late in the year, you're lucky to get one new player a pack, and there were still six more to go. I stuck the cards under my legs for a second, and wiped my sweaty hands on my pants. I looked out the window. Students were just starting to leave O'Connor. That meant it was three o'clock.

I thought I'd rest for a bit. When something's really exciting, like a good book or opening a new pack, sometimes you want to slow down and make it last. When our family was coming back from our big trip two years ago, I remember hoping that the car would run out of gas or break down, or we'd pick up a hitchhiker going the opposite way, anything to make the trip longer. I could recognize more and more things as we got closer to Edmonton, and I was afraid that once we got back I'd start forgetting all the great things on the trip, so I was trying as hard as I could to memorize them. Everybody else was homesick and counting down the miles, and I couldn't understand why. The funny thing was, once we were home, I was glad to be there, and I didn't forget the holiday stuff, either. I got the best of both.

Before getting back at the cards, I took another look up at Sister. She was still busy correcting essays or something. A few people were losing their concentration or were finished, so things were getting a bit noisier. I figured I'd be okay with the cards, because the minute Sister lifts her head, things always go quiet. That would be my cue to put the cards away and get back to the multiplication questions.

Here we go, I thought. Next card. No way! Unbelievable!! Rod Carew, Twins. A new card, an all-star, and a batting champion, all in one. The guy Ted Williams says will be the next .400 hitter, and now I had him. This was a pack in a million, and I was only halfway through. I couldn't wait to show Keith.

Next card. Rusty Staub, Expos. Got him, but it was still neat to see the card. It reminded me of how exciting it was two years ago when Montreal came into the majors, Canada's first team. Me and Dad watched their very first home game, against the Mets, on TV. Jarry Park looked small and embarrassing compared to a place like Yankee Stadium, and those red, white and blue Expos caps looked like kids' beanies, even on a black-and-white TV, but still, they were our team, and Rusty Staub was their first big star. Whenever he came up to the plate the public address guy would shout out 'Le Grand Orange!' That means the big orange. At first I couldn't understand why they were naming him after a fruit, but later Dad explained it was because his hair was red.

Card number seven. Carl Yastrzemski, Red Sox. Got him, but another future Hall of Famer, so I'd keep it. He's also the first player I remember seeing on TV, in 1967, when Boston won the pennant. That was Canada's Centennial year, too. There were all these birthday celebrations on. On July 1, they cut a giant birthday cake on Parliament Hill in Ottawa, right by the bank where Mum had her first big city job. As soon as the cake was cut, Dad flipped channels. There was supposed to be a game on, but the Centennial stuff was on all three channels. Finally, about an hour later, the game was joined in progress. It was the Red Sox and somebody else. Yastrzemski came to the plate, and when they flashed his name I thought it must be some mistake. How were you supposed say that? It was even weirder in the box scores in the paper, where they shortened it to Ystrzmsk. Dad said most people just called him Yaz. No wonder. When Boston went to the Series that year, I thought that meant that every team I ever cheered for would always win. It hasn't exactly turned out that way. Look at the Expos. And the Leafs.

Just before flipping to the eighth card, I realized that a little problem was developing. The gumstick on the roof of my mouth was turning all soft and runny. My mouth was getting filled with all this sugary gob. But I was still afraid that if I started chewing it would be too loud and slurpy. Nothing gets Sister's goat worse than somebody chewing gum in class. The last guy to get caught, Orest Tymchuk, had to write the words 'slovenly' and 'disrespectful' two hundred times on the blackboard after school. I had to try to pretty much keep my mouth shut and breathe through my nose for the rest of the class. I looked at the clock. Twenty more minutes.

The eighth card turned out to be one of those rip-off, waste ones. It was an index card, where you check off the ones you've already got. That's completely feeble, because everybody I know who collects cards knows exactly which ones they've got without looking at some stupid index. You get to the point where you can practically smell a new card. The only thing an index card is good for is jimmying a lock. I had to do that once when I came back late from a pop bottle drive and everybody had gone to church. I felt like Inspector Clouseau, breaking into my own place. When they got back, Mum and Dad weren't really mad, I think because they thought we were collecting the bottles for charity or something. Actually, me and Keith and Freddy bought records and chocolate bars. That's the time I got 'Neanderthal Man' by Hotlegs.

I was daydreaming like that when I flipped to the ninth card, so I didn't look down at it right away. I thought about pop bottles, which made me think about Keith's dad, who worked in a pop bottle factory. They put Orange Crush in bottles there. They always used to have tons of it at Puzniaks' place. Keith said his dad got it for free. You'd go over there and everybody would have orange moustaches, and orange stains on their teeth. They'd hand you a bottle before you even got in the door. It was great. That was before Mr Puzniak got fired. Then I got thinking of Keith's baba, and living in holes and not speaking English. I guess I got pretty deep into the daydream. I can't think of why else I wouldn't have noticed at first what Daniela was doing in the next row. She said later she did it quite a few times. What she was doing was leaning over a bit, and, with her arm down low, sort of poking me in the leg. For a second I was thinking, 'Wow,

Daniela's tickling me!' By the time I looked over at her, her hand was back on her desk, and her eyes were on her paper. Then I noticed there was a shadow next to my desk, a shadow that wasn't normally there.

I looked up. Sister Arlene was standing right over me.

SIXTEEN

You hear stories about people seeing their whole life flash by
when they think they're going to die. I saw a war movie once
where a soldier, as he was lying bleeding on the battlefield, went
back to his baby voice and started crying 'Mommy! Mommy! I'm
hungry!' I have to admit I didn't do that when I saw Sister
standing there, though. I mean, of course I knew I was in it pretty
deep, but the weird thing was, I wasn't thinking about what she'd
yell, or about going to Mr Horvath's office and getting the strap,
or even about what Mum and Dad would think. All I kept
thinking was 'Two more. There's still two more cards in the
pack. She can't take them, because I haven't seen the whole pack
yet.'

But she did take them. She just held out her hand. It looked
more like a lumberjack's hand than a nun's, all big and leathery.
Sister must have done some hard work in her life. There was no
use resisting, so I put the cards in her hand. She still hadn't said
anything. She didn't have to. By now the room was so quiet you
could hear the second hand on the clock ticking. When Sister
finally said something, it sure wasn't what I expected. Her voice
was soft.

– Blasphemy.

She was looking down at the top card, the one I hadn't quite
looked at, when she said it. All the blood was draining from her
face. Now I really was getting scared. 'Blasphemy' is about the
worst word you could hear from a nun teacher. It means making
fun of God, or doing something so disrespectful that God would
take it personally. I heard Mum say it once, when we saw some
spraypainting on the side of an old church in Ontario. But I
couldn't figure out what baseball cards had to do with blasphemy.
Sure, I shouldn't have been looking at them in class, but I
couldn't understand what made that so much worse than other
things you could get caught doing, like picking your nose or
plagiarism. Then she turned the card over and looked at the back.
Her face got even whiter and her eyes even bigger.

– *Blasphemy!!*

This time she really shouted it. By now there were tears in my eyes. I just didn't get it. I couldn't let myself cry, though, because a bunch of pink, gobby drool would have come pouring out the sides of my mouth. Already I could feel bits of it trickling out one side. After what felt like forever, Sister turned the card around and held it in my face. Slowly I started to understand.

It was Jesus Alou. He's an outfielder for the Houston Astros. He's got two other brothers in the majors, Matty and Felipe. They've all hit .300. Matty even won the batting championship once, with Pittsburgh. Anyway, Sister wasn't shouting 'Blasphemy!' about anything to do with baseball. It's not like she was a Reds fan who cheered against the Astros or something. What got her so upset was the name, Jesus. Actually, it's a pretty popular name in countries where they speak Spanish, like the Dominican Republic, where the Alou brothers are from. You don't even pronounce it the normal way. You're supposed to say it more like 'Hey, Seuss.' But Sister didn't know all that. She must have thought Jesus was a nickname for this guy or something. I also figured out why the back of the card got her even madder. On the back of every card, with the player's statistics and where he was born and stuff, there's a little cartoon and a personal fact about the player. You'll see stuff like 'Bob played football in high school' or 'Lefty enjoys fishing in the off-season.' Well, on the back of this card, I remembered, there was a little drawing of a guy in a baseball cap playing in a band, with musical notes floating around. The caption said 'Jesus likes to play the organ.' That's what made Sister lose it.

So now I knew why Sister was so mad, and I knew she was wrong, but that wasn't helping. There was no way I was going to explain the stuff about Spanish people naming their sons Jesus. You could tell by the look on her face that Sister wouldn't even have heard. So all I could really do was just sit there and wait for whatever the punishment was going to be to be over with. It was like sitting in the waiting room at the dentist, except the dentist doesn't usually drill you in front of thirty kids.

– What is this filth? she asked.

What was I supposed to say? It was one of those questions you're not really expected to answer, and I couldn't have opened my mouth to talk even if I'd wanted to. So I just sort of shrugged. Jesus Alou, with his bat on his shoulder and a wad of chewing tobacco in one cheek, was still staring me in the face.

– Don't interrupt, Sister said.

I wasn't going to.

– This ... this ... I cannot find words. This is a disgrace. It is an affront and an insult to all I hold dear. It is one thing to bring your childish ... *hobbies* ... into this place of learning, and to squander your intelligence on such trifles when there is ... learning, to be done. It is quite another to desecrate our school with this ... this ... thing, this thing that takes the name of our ... no. This I cannot forgive. I simply cannot forgive.

I still couldn't look her in the eyes. Finally she turned around and walked up to her desk, holding the cards out away from her body like she was scared they'd contaminate her or something. She put them down on a corner of her desk like they put down pieces of evidence in a courtroom, then turned around and faced the class.

– No one is to move, nor to make any sound louder than the scrape of a pencil on paper, until I return, she said.

Then she walked out the door. It wasn't too hard to guess where she was going. Mr Horvath's office. Normally a teacher will send a bad kid straight to the office, or wait until the end of the class and take him down, but I guess this was a special case, being a blasphemy, or maybe Sister was just so mad she wasn't thinking straight.

So there we were, sitting in a classroom with no teacher, and everybody but me and maybe Daniela having no idea what really just happened. People were looking at me in lots of different ways. Lots were all bug-eyed with their jaws hanging open. Some, like Leslie Gibson and Freddy, had little smiles on their faces like they thought I must have done something cool, and others had that man-are-you-gonna-get-it smile. Nobody said anything. Some time while I sat there watching people watch me, I must have remembered that I could chew my gum now, because I opened my mouth and started slurping the pink gob around. A big gasp went up, like at the circus when the trapeze lady almost falls.

All this time, it's kind of hard to explain how I felt. It was like there were two mes. One was all shaking and scared, with the word 'Blasphemy!' ringing in his ears. The other was the 'One more card' guy, trying to think of how to see which player it was. I mean, you can't open a pack and not see every player that's in it. That would be like having your dessert grabbed away after dinner, or drawing a picture of somebody and not bothering with the head.

The one-more-card voice must have been louder than the other one, because pretty soon I realized that I was trying to think of ways to get the pack back. I stared at them up on Sister's desk, and tried to work out how long it would take her to go to the office and back. I had a pretty good idea how long that was, because the bathroom the boys use when we need to go to the can is down across the hall from the office. It takes about three to five minutes to go there, and back, depending on how long your leak or your job is.

I looked up at the clock. It was twenty after three. Ten more minutes till the last bell, and probably five more until Sister got back with Mr Horvath, or some giant strap, or the police, or whatever. I made my decision. I had to get the pack back. I had to see that last card.

Once I knew what I was going to do, it got a lot easier. Maybe I knew that I was in it so deep already that it couldn't really get any worse. I don't know. All I knew was, I was closing my arithmetic scribbler, putting it with the other Duo-Tangs in a pile, sticking my pencil inside it, and standing up. I went up to Sister's desk, feeling not quite real, like I was watching myself in a movie. I could feel everybody's eyes on me. I took the cards, stuck them in my pocket, and headed for the door. Just before I stepped out, I glanced back at the class. I saw Freddy giving me the black power salute, Brad and Leslie and Victor smiling, and Carl Wysocki crying. I also saw Daniela just staring, with a look on her face that was hard to make out.

Out in the hallway, it was like I was somebody in one of those What's Wrong with This Picture? puzzles. The building and the hallway were right, but the clock was wrong. It should have said 3:30, not 3:20. The number of kids in the hall was also wrong. There should have been hundreds, but instead there was just one. Me.

The way to the office, where Sister would be coming back from, was to the right. Lucky for me, our classroom was right by a stairwell and exit to the left. I turned that way, without looking back, went through the stairwell doors, and started walking down. The calm feeling I'd had a minute before was fading now, though, and my knees started shaking so bad I could hardly walk. I kept my eyes on my feet and my hand on the banister to steady myself. Halfway down, I bumped into what looked at first like a hairy dog, but turned out to be a mop. I looked up and Mr Nedved, the janitor, was standing there, not really mopping, just leaning on the handle and humming a song I didn't recognize. At first I was worried he might stop me and ask why I was leaving early, but instead he just nodded, stepped aside, and kept on humming. I took the bottom flight of stairs two steps at a time, and threw myself through the exit doors onto the sidewalk outside.

SEVENTEEN

It was so much brighter outside than in that I was blinded for a minute. All the gold leaves and brown grass and the red brick school across the street made a kind of giant rusty screen in front of my eyes. Bit by bit things got clearer, and pretty soon I could see a long line of yellow school buses waiting for 3:30, when everybody would pour out of the school. Between the buses I could see through to the O'Connor football field, where the team was practising. There was the sound of coaches yelling and helmets cracking together. Off to the right I could hear organ music coming out the open doors of St Paul's church. Father Nolan must have been working on a hymn. He's pretty good.

Without really thinking, I turned right, spat out my gum, and headed for this little spot between the doors and the playground. It's just this little gravel space up against the school, partly hidden by a tree. It's usually full of gum wrappers and cigarette butts, and has dirty words and pictures drawn on the walls. Grade sixes hang out there at recess, and I think the janitors go there for smokes sometimes. It seemed like a good place for me to calm down and check out that last card. So I ducked in under a branch. I was just starting to pull the pack out of my pocket when a voice scared me out of my shorts.

– Step into my office, man. Want a drag?

It was Tommy Winchester. He was sitting on the gravel with his back against the wall, holding out a lit cigarette.

– No, thanks, I said.

I said it like it was the most normal thing in the world, for two grade fours to be hanging around right outside the school, in class hours, and one of them offering the other one a smoke. Ho hum. Actually, it was probably the weirdest situation I've ever been in.

– What are you doing here? I asked.

– I think the question is, what are *you* doing here? I come here a lot. I kind of like this little place.

He had a point about why was I there. Tommy skips quite a

bit. In fact, he's pretty much the only kid in the school who skips at all. I didn't notice him missing from arithmetic, but I guess that's because it was nothing unusual. But I was doing it for the first time.

– I had some trouble with Sister, I said.

– Hey, man, join the club.

I was getting nervous about 3:30 getting so close. In a minute there'd be hundreds of students passing just on the other side of the tree, some of them probably looking for me.

– Hey, man, I've got an idea, Tommy said.

– Yeah? What?

– Wanna come to my place? We can hang out. I'll play you some records. Tull, Sabbath, Zeppelin, Stones.

I couldn't think of a good reason to say no right at that minute. Plus, it was giving me the creeps being in that little space. The smell of pee was getting stronger.

– Sure, I said.

– Cool.

We left the smelly space and headed out between two school buses, across 132nd. We had to swerve around the football field to keep from getting creamed by big guys with shoulder pads.

The Winchesters live in the row housing between the field and 82nd Street. I'd only been there once before, for Wade Two Feathers's birthday party. It's a bit of a scary place. It's poorer than the row housing where Keith and Victor and those guys live. Most of the back yards have nothing in them, not even fences between them. Here and there you see big rusty cars propped up on bricks, with guys working underneath them. Most of the men you see look pretty much the same, with long hair and baseball caps and packs of smokes tucked under their shirt sleeves. The women look the same, only with longer hair. Little kids with dirty faces are always playing around, and lots of mean-looking dogs are chained to the laundry poles.

It only took a minute to get to Tommy's place. On the way, I had a weird thought. I realized that all my best friends lived in the other direction from school, over on the way to my place. It's been that way ever since kindergarten. It makes you think, how much your life depends on where you happen to live. If our house was on Tommy's side of the school, closer to 82nd, I might have had completely different friends and done different things. I stopped thinking about that when we got to Tommy's front door.

– Step right in, man, Tommy said.

The door wasn't locked, so I thought somebody must be home, but as soon as we went in I could tell nobody was. Somehow you can just feel when a house is empty. It was weird for me, because I can't ever remember a time when Mum wasn't there when I got home.

– Be right back, man. Gotta drain the weasel. Make yourself comfortable, Tommy said.

As Tommy went upstairs to the can, I could hear the St Paul's buzzer ringing off in the distance. It sounded a lot further away than it really was. While Tommy was gone, I had a few minutes to look around and get used to the place. That was a good thing, because it took some getting used to.

The first place I looked was the record rack. It's a habit I have whenever I go in a new place. Most people's parents, if they have records at all, have stuff like Herb Alpert and the Tijuana Brass, or James Last party records, and soundtracks like *My Fair Lady* and *The Sound of Music*. The records here were more like stuff my older brothers and sisters might get, and some stuff I hadn't even heard of. There were a bunch of Bob Dylan albums, some by a guy who looked like Dylan called Phil Ochs, two by Country Joe and the Fish, and some blues records by guys with names like Muddy and Sonny Boy. I thought, this is a place where you could play records without your parents telling you to turn them down.

Next I looked at the books. That wasn't hard, because they were everywhere, stacked on shelves against every wall, piled on the floor, even crammed into the little closet by the door. You could tell they'd been read, too. They all had that thumbed-through look. I saw some big ones with names like *Anthropology Today* and *Advanced Criminology*. I knew Tommy's parents were in university, or at least trying to get in. This must have been what they were studying, stuff about primitive tribes and criminals. That explained why Tommy always had copies of *Man, Myth and Magic*.

I didn't notice at first, but the place was pretty messy, with socks and magazines on the floor. The furniture was interesting, too. There wasn't much of it, and it looked like the kind of stuff you see at garage sales, with missing legs and cigarette burns. That didn't bug me, though. The place seemed more like one big messy bedroom than somebody's house where you're afraid to blow your nose. I liked that. What did kind of freak me out was the last thing I saw before Tommy came back down from the can. It was these two big posters, on opposite sides of the living room. One was of a gigantic peace sign, with 'Footprint of the American Chicken' written underneath. I think that was a joke. The other was a big picture from that movie *Easy Rider*. I haven't seen it, but Susan and Duncan have told me about it. It's about motorcycle hippies, kind of like those ones we saw in New York State. The poster showed a guy zooming along on his chopper, but the weird part was that he was giving the camera the finger. You could see it plain as day. This was right on the living room wall.

I must have been really staring at that finger, because I didn't notice Tommy until he was right behind my shoulder. When he spoke, it made me jump.

– Born to be wild, man.

– Yeah, I said. Neat.

I still couldn't believe it. A guy giving the finger on your living room wall. How could you have company over?

– Wild movie, man, Tommy said. You know what happens about half a second after this picture?

– What?

– A redneck in a pick-up blows the dude's brains out. Double barrel shotgun. Pow! The end, man.

I wasn't sure what a redneck was. It sounded like some kind of bird, but that was impossible. I figured I'd look it up later.

All this standing around looking at strange things was getting to me a bit. I must have been feeling the need for something more normal, because I started looking around for the TV. I couldn't see one.

– Where's your TV? I asked.

– We don't have one, man.

– You mean you haven't bought one yet since you moved here?

– No, I mean we just don't have one. Never have. My old man and lady say it rots your brain.

– But don't you ever feel like watching things? Sports and stuff?

– Hey, man, you can't miss what you've never had. Anyway, do I look like a sports fan? Rah, rah, home team? Try again, man.

No TV, no sports. That still left music.

– You must listen to lots of records, then, I said.

– Yeah. I mean, I don't have lots, but the ones I have, I listen to all the time. Let's play some now, man.

– Sure.

I headed to the pile of Dylans and stuff.

– Not those, man, Tommy said. I don't dig all that folkie stuff. I like head music, man. The heavy stuff. Follow me, if you dare.

He headed through a door into the basement. I went after. It was really dark down there. The only light was from one bare bulb. The windows were those thick kind you can't really see through, like on shower doors. The only furniture was a mattress on the floor, with a dresser and a little all-in-one stereo next to it. No washer or dryer. We went to the mattress, and sort of half sat, half lay on it. Tommy pulled an album from a pile of about ten. It was the Black Sabbath one he showed me at recess that time. I looked at the name. *Paranoid.* Weird.

– Lie down and dig this, man, Tommy said.

He dropped the needle, went over and turned out the one light, and came back and lay down next to me on the mattress. When the music started, something sounded wrong. It sounded like a 45 on 33 or something. The guitar was all slow and groany, like a moose call almost, and it took forever for the singer to come in. When he did, he had a whiny voice. The words were something about war and pigs. It was hard to make them out. I kept waiting for the catchy part, the part that you could sing along with, to come. Every song has one, I thought. But these ones didn't seem to.

It went on for quite a while, these long groany songs playing while we lay there staring into the dark. I could hear Tommy making drum and guitar sounds, and sometimes singing some of the lyrics. I tried, but I just wasn't getting it. The whole thing was creeping me out a bit. After what felt like an hour but must have been only about twenty minutes, the first side ended. It was one of those stereos where you have to pick up the needle yourself, but it took Tommy a minute to do it. He was still lying there making guitar sounds.

– Was that wild or what, man? he asked.

– I guess.

– You guess what?

– I mean, I guess it was wild. I didn't really get it.

– Get it? What's there to get? You've just got to let it wash over you, man. It's a trip.

– I guess.

– Oh, man, you guess, you guess. Let me ask you something.

– Yeah?

– What do you think music is *for*?

– For?

– Yeah, man. I know you're into music. Why do you listen to it?

I'd never really thought about it.

– I don't know, I said. I mean, I know, but it's hard to explain.

– I'm all ears, man.

– Well, I guess because it makes me feel better.

– What, you mean *happier*? It makes you *dance* and *sing*?

He said it like those were the stupidest things in the world, but I didn't see what was so wrong with them.

– Yeah, I said. But not just that. Music, when it's good, I don't know, it's like it takes you somewhere else. When a Beatles song, like 'Strawberry Fields' comes on the radio, it puts all these pictures in your mind. It makes you feel like you're walking on air, or floating in space.

We lay in the dark, not saying anything for a minute, before Tommy answered.

– Hey, man, that's cool. I can dig that. Different strokes. It's just different music that does it for me, man. And you can't get it on the radio.

He was right about that. It's hard to imagine Black Sabbath on CHED, between Donny Osmond and Carole King. I was still feeling a bit frustrated about his music question, though. I didn't think my answer was all that good. It's hard. You can't really talk about music. I mean, you can talk about instruments and stuff, and the difference between, say, Beethoven and the Zombies, but I don't know if you can really explain why you like one song more than another, or why the Beatles are better than, I don't know, Grand Funk Railroad. I mean, of course they are. Anyone with half a brain can see that. But it's tough to say in words.

– Maybe Tull's a bit more up your alley, man, Tommy said.

He was talking about Jethro Tull, the guy with the flute. I've looked at his album covers in Scotty's at Northgate. He's really weird. He stands on one leg, and wears these sort of leotards, with a cup over his thing, like they do in those Shakespeare movies. I was kind of curious to hear how he sounded.

– Sure. Put it on, I said.

I thought Tommy would have had to turn the light back on to change records, but he didn't. I guess he's trained himself to see like a bat down there, because he did it all in the dark. Pretty soon the Tull record started. It was weird, too, but in a different way from Black Sabbath. This time, the music was all fast and fancy, part electric and part acoustic. The beat kept changing, so you never knew how to tap your foot. The main guy, Jethro, sounded like he was singing with a clothespin on his nose, and when he played his flute, he did this sort of snort every time he took a breath. It's exactly what they teach you not to do in flute lessons.

– *This* is music, man. Tull's a genius, Tommy said.

I didn't say anything. A minute later, Tommy all of a sudden sat up.

– We're forgetting something very important, man.

He started rooting around between the mattress and the basement wall, and pulled up something. I couldn't see what it was. Then I heard a little switch flick, and a light came on. It was a flashlight. I could have asked Tommy why he didn't just turn the regular light back on, but I didn't bother.

– Come and check this out, man, he said.

He walked across the basement, shining the light in front of him. I followed. On the far wall he got to this thing, I think it was a fuse box, and opened the little door on it. On the bottom ledge there was this little metal box, kind of like the thing my Mum keeps her rare coin collection in. It was locked with a tiny padlock. Tommy felt around in some cobwebs at the back and pulled out a bobby pin. He used that to pick the lock, and opened up the box.

– Abracadabra, he said.

He shone the light into the box and held it out so I could see. There was this brown lumpy thing that looked like a little dried turd, a plastic bag with some green stuff in it, and some little pieces of paper that looked like mini napkins or something. I had no idea what was going on.

– What is it? I asked.

– It's my old man's stash, man.

– His what?

– His stash, man. His little treasure chest. Top grade Acapulco Gold.

– Gold?

– *Weed*, man. Mary Jane. Merry Wanna. Got it?

– Yeah.

I'd never really seen it before, only pictures of people smoking it, and those hippies in Saranac Lake. I pictured it looking a lot more leafy.

– You haven't heard music until you've heard it on this stuff, man, Tommy said.

He took a couple of papers and a little pinch of the green stuff, shut the box, and put it back in the fuse box. Then he shone the flashlight back in the direction of the mattress, and headed over there. I followed him. What else was I supposed to do? We sat on the mattress, with the flashlight on the floor shining up at us. We made huge monstery shadows on the wall behind us. Tommy pulled a broken half of an ordinary cigarette out of his pocket, knocked out the tobacco, and put it on the two little papers in his lap. Then he put the green stuff in, and mixed it in. Finally, he licked a bit of each paper, and rolled them into little cigarette shapes. The whole thing only took a minute.

– Puff the magic dragon, man, Tommy said.

Then he pulled a lighter out of his pocket, lit one up, and turned off the flashlight. The only light in the room was the little glow from the end of the thing.

– Is that a joint? I asked.

– Hey, man, you're hipper than you look. Yes, this is a joint. Back home, in Berkeley, they called them doobies, or funny cigarettes.

He put it in his mouth and took a long hard suck, the same

way I've seen him do with regular cigarettes. He held the smoke in his mouth until I thought his eyes would pop out. Finally, he let the smoke out slowly, partly from his mouth and partly through his nose. When he talked again, his voice sounded funny, kind of deeper.

– I just don't understand …

He stopped for a second and blew out even more smoke. I couldn't believe there was still some in his mouth. By now there was a big cloud of it around us.

– I just don't understand why this stuff is illegal, man. Let me tell you something. If everybody used this, there'd be no wars in the world. Give some to Nixon, man, and presto, no more Vietnam. Did you know …

He sniffed some of the smoke in the air. Some of it was getting into my nose and mouth, too.

– Did you know, there's these cats in Jamaica who use this stuff as, like, a holy sacrament?

– I didn't know that, I said.

– I kid you not, man. These dudes get together out in the bush, pound on a big drum, and sing sacred songs for days while they toke. They say it gets them in touch with God. Saw it in *Man, Myth and Magic*, man. Wild.

He did the sucking and holding his breath thing again, and leaned over to turn up the music even louder. Then, after he blew the smoke out, he held the joint out to me.

– What? I said.

– Share the bounty, man. Take a toke.

– I don't know.

– You don't know what?

– I mean, I've never smoked. I don't know how.

– Nothing to it, man. Just suck, hold and blow. If you know how to breathe, you know how to toke.

I was starting to panic a bit. I could feel my armpits, and around my gaunch, getting wet with sweat. It was partly my fear of fire, partly the 'illegal' thing, partly the creepy light and flutey music. Plus, and I'm not sure about this, I think the smoke was starting to get me a bit, you know, stoned. I was feeling a bit dizzy, and funny shapes were forming in the darkness. The music was getting, not better exactly, but at least more interesting. I could hear every instrument really clearly, like they were coming from different corners of the room, and the flute, for some reason, was making me see a giant pterodactyl swooping around the room. I had to duck a couple of times to get out of its way. I looked over at Tommy. He was still holding the joint in front of my face. The sparks were making swirly firefly lines in the air.

– Umm, I'll try it in a minute, I said.

– In a minute?

– Yeah. I've gotta take a leak.

– Sure, man. I'm not going anywhere. Top floor, on your left.

– Thanks.

Tommy held out the flashlight so I could see the basement door, and I opened it and started going up the stairs. At first, I just stood there, because the stairs looked like they were going up themselves, like an escalator. I hung on tight to the handrail. After a while, I'm not sure how long, I looked up and saw I wasn't getting any closer to the top. It wasn't an escalator after all. I made my way up, got a bit lost on the main floor, and finally found the stairs to go up. Once I got to the top, I stopped a bit to let my head clear.

I have to admit, I never really had to take a leak. I just made that up to get out of the basement for a while. So there I was, standing outside the bathroom door, not having to go. I looked down the hall and saw two open doors. I thought, I've come up all this way, why not have a look? I know it's snooping, but it was hard to resist. Besides, you get the idea that the Winchesters aren't people who care a whole lot about what other people think. I mean, come on, they've got a guy giving the finger on their living room wall.

The first door I looked in must have been to Mr and Mrs Winchester's bedroom. Just like in the basement, it was pretty bare, with a mattress on the floor instead of an ordinary bed, and an antique-looking dresser. There were some posters on the walls up here, too. One showed a soldier, who looked like he'd just been shot a split second before, with the word 'Why?' in big letters underneath. Another one was a huge closeup of a guy's face. He looked a bit like Jesus, with a beard and one of those funny caps like they wear in France. All it said was 'Che'. I think he's a rock star from Spain.

Next I looked into the room across the hall. It had another ton of books, maybe even more than downstairs, and a big desk with a chair at each end. It looked like Tommy's folks did their studying and writing in here, sometimes at the same time. I glanced at some of the books, and noticed something weird. Lots of them were in Spanish, and some of them were in some other language, with a different, upside-down looking alphabet. It might have been Russian. I also noticed a few pictures on the walls, and in little frames on the desk, and took a closer look. One of them showed a guy at a microphone, with really long hair and nerd glasses like people wore a few years ago. A bunch of people were behind him waving signs saying things like 'What are we doing in Vietnam?' and 'LBJ's a Baby Killer'. The guy at the microphone was Tommy's dad. His hair's even longer now, but I could tell it was him. Next to that was another frame with a newspaper clipping in it. It showed two people being dragged along by the hair and feet, by a bunch of cops. There were other cops in the background on horses. I leaned a little closer, and what I saw gave me goosebumps. The two people getting dragged by the cops were Mr and Mrs Winchester. The headline under the photo said 'Six Injured, Four Arrested at Anti-Draft Rally'.

I stood in the middle of that room for a minute. All I could think of was how different Tommy's life was from mine. I mean, there we were in the same school, with the same teachers, living in the same neighbourhood in the same city and country, but really we might as well have been on different planets.

It was right around then that a funny feeling started coming over me, sort of like what you get in an elevator that's going down too fast. Maybe it was all that weird stuff catching up with me all at once – the finger poster, the weird music, the marijuana smoke, the picture of parents getting arrested. I could hear the flute music all the way from the basement. I even thought I smelled the druggy smoke coming up through the heating vent. Whatever it was, all of a sudden I felt a huge puke coming on. The last thing I wanted to do was toss my cookies all over somebody's books and stuff, so I ran as fast as I could to the bathroom, with the puke halfway up my throat. I didn't quite get to the can on time. I mean, mostly I hit the toilet bowl, but some of it missed and landed on the rim and the floor around the can. It was enough to make you puke just looking at it.

As I kneeled there on my knees in front of the can, I remember thinking that I'd never had my head inside a toilet bowl before. The little letters inside said 'Armitage Shanks'. It sounded like the name of some basketball player. I thought about toilets, how many there must be in the world, how many millions of people at that very minute were taking a leak or dropping a log. I remembered a picture I saw once in *Life* magazine, of a building right after an earthquake, or maybe a bomb. One whole wall was missing, and you could see into every room, like a dollhouse. In the bathroom, the toilet was sitting right on a ledge, three floors up. It looked like if anybody sat on it, it would fall right over. I've had a few dreams about that picture. Our family is in that house, and every time somebody has to go to the can, they have to decide if it's worth the risk of sitting on that toilet, and maybe falling three floors down.

I realized that I couldn't just kneel there forever. Sooner or later I was going to have to stand up, and clean up the mess. But as I looked around, I couldn't see any towels or facecloths or things to clean with. I checked the toilet paper roll, and there was only one little sheet left. That wouldn't go far. I thought for a second about using my shirt, but how was I going to explain that to Mum? 'Well, Mum, I was at the Winchesters' place, and I must have breathed a little too much marijuana smoke, because I hurled all over the can.' I don't think so. Going down and telling Tommy about it didn't seem like such a hot idea either, for some reason. I'd just have to find a way to clean up myself.

Staring at my puke trying to come up with some brilliant idea for making it disappear wasn't getting me anywhere, so I turned around, and what I saw made me scream. It was another poster, on the wall in front of the toilet. Boy, these people were really into posters. This one was of Frank Zappa, that rock star who they say peed on his audience once. The poster showed him sitting on a toilet, with his pants down around his ankles. On top, in big letters, it said 'Phi Zappa Krappa'.

I kind of gawked at that poster for a while, not because it was that weird, but more because of where it was. It's the kind of thing you might expect to see in some teenage boy's bedroom or hippie record store, but in an ordinary bathroom? I mean, this is what Tommy and his parents would be staring at every single time they sat on the can. Not to mention anybody else who happened to use their bathroom, like me. Was I the only person who'd ever visited here or something? Both answers to that question, yes or no, were things I didn't really want to hear.

What I did next wasn't just because of the Zappa poster. That was just the last thing to push me. I think it was really because of all the things I'd seen in that house, or even all the weird things that had been happening all day. All I knew was, I had to get out of that place. I couldn't stay a minute longer. I felt pretty bad about the mess, and about just leaving Tommy down in the basement, but I didn't see what else I could do. I was afraid if I looked once more at the mess I'd puke again, so I didn't. I left the bathroom, went down the stairs, picked up my school books from the crooked couch, and turned to leave. The music was still blasting from the basement, and the marijuana smell was all over the house by now. Before I had a chance to change my mind, I took off out the front door. The last thing I saw was the guy on the chopper giving me the finger.

The row of houses where the Winchesters live doesn't have a street in front of it. Cars have to go in by the back alley. The front yard just keeps going. It turns into the O'Connor football field, which turns into a park that goes past the playschool and the outdoor rink and Glengarry Daycare. If I wanted to, I could go almost all the way home on grass. I ran for a bit, then turned back to look at Tommy's place. I thought he might be on the step yelling for me or something, but he wasn't. I got this picture in my head of Tommy still being down there years from now, still puffing on his Dad's stash and listening to head music in the dark. It's like those stories you hear about old Japanese guys who still don't know the war is over. They're hiding out in jungles on islands in the South Pacific, all this time later, waiting until it's safe to come out. I'm not sure why Tommy reminds me of them. He's actually a pretty nice guy, even if he smokes too much.

EIGHTEEN

I sat on the grass by the running track for a while, pulling out blades and eating the white roots. The football team's practice was just ending. Players were pulling off their helmets and carrying tackling dummies back inside. The coach was yelling stuff.

– Come on, men! Five o'clock! Let's look sharp!

It took a minute to sink in. Five o'clock. The memory came back to me of Mum, way back at lunchtime, telling me to be sure to come straight back from school. Yikes. Five o'clock was not exactly straight back. She'd be mad, or worried, or both. I got up and started heading home, past the O'Connor garage where they have automotives classes, and over to the playground where I used to hang out before grade one. It's weird going back to an old playground. Everything is so small. You bump your head in places where you used to fit.

As I was walking I coughed and realized my breath was still a bit pukey, so I stopped to gargle with some water from the drinking fountain, the same one Duncan told me not to drink from because you could get tapeworms from it. Stepping back down from the fountain, I felt that poking feeling on my leg again. The baseball cards. That made twice in one day I'd forgotten all about them. Something weird was definitely happening to me. Two hours before, I'd done something that could get me expelled from school, just to get the cards back, and then I didn't even bother looking at them.

Before I could think too much about the trouble I was in at school, I pulled the cards out, to see what the last one was. Card number ten, Joe Torre, Cardinals. He's been leading the league in hitting all year, and he's got amazing eyebrows, but I already had him. Still, a pretty good pack, even if I still didn't have Clemente. If I hadn't seen Chris's Clemente, I might have stopped believing that there really was one.

Putting the cards back in my pocket, and keeping on walking, I had this funny feeling. I realized that I didn't seem to care as much about the cards any more. I mean, I was still happy about getting such a great pack, and still sad about the Clemente thing, but it didn't feel like a matter of life and death any more. What made me do what I did, grabbing them and leaving school like that? Weird.

I was only about a block from home when I looked up and froze for a minute. I was practically right in front of the Santuccis' place. They live in the same row housing as Keith, but closer to our place. Usually you see a zillion kids' trikes and croquet mallets and stuff in their front yard, but today there was nothing. It was all neat and mowed. Somehow that made me even more scared to pass, and maybe get seen and beat up. But I didn't have much choice. The only other way home would have been a big detour, and I was already so late. So I walked by, real slow, rehearsing what I'd say if Tony came out to attack me. It was like walking past an invisible snarly dog. I didn't want anybody to smell my fear, like dogs can do. They only bite scared people. Some dogs, though, like Sam, just lick and sniff and hump everybody exactly the same.

I got by the Santuccis' okay, crossed the street, and went down the pathway between the Pippigs' and the Vrbaks'. It's funny how I never went home the front way. I practically never saw the front yard.

As soon as I turned into the back yard, I knew something was different. It was a bit like the feeling of going into Tommy's empty place, only the opposite. Lots of people were home. I could tell by all the voices coming from inside. That was weird, because everybody's never home together at the same time except for special occasions, and sometimes not even then. Howard will be off at some construction job, Susan and Anne will be off with boyfriends, Duncan and Richard will be at some sports practice. Lots of times it's just me, Mary and Mum, until Dad gets home around 5:30. But today everybody was there. Maybe it's some kind of party, I thought.

I opened the back screen door, and just stopped, half in and half out. Everything looked so different that for a second I thought I had the wrong house, but it was definitely the right one because these were my brothers and sisters and parents and dog in it.

What I saw was boxes and pop crates everywhere, and everybody buzzing around, putting stuff in them and stuffing them with newspapers. The cupboard over the kitchen counter was open, but instead of Rice Krispies and graham wafers in it, there was nothing. I went to put my books on the kitchen table. It wasn't there. Neither was the chair I went to sit on. I felt like I did when me and Keith used to go the wrong way on the escalators at Woodward's. No matter where I stood, I was in somebody's way. Nobody even asked why I was so late getting home from school. I guess they were too busy to notice. But what were they doing? What was going on? I still didn't really get it.

I sort of sidestepped through the kitchen and turned into the living room. The rug was all rolled up, and you could see the hardwood floor. It was the first time that floor wasn't covered since I was about four. It was a really big deal when we got that rug, and covered the hardwood. All the neighbours came over to ooh and ahh at it. It meant we weren't poor any more.

Looking around in all directions, not one thing was the same. One thing that really hit me was a framed picture, leaning on the wall on the floor in a corner. Above it was the spot where it always used to hang, darker than the rest of the wall around it. The picture was of this great big blue heron, flying through a swamp, with the trees and bird reflected upside down in the water. Mum said it was by one of the Group of Seven, these famous Canadian artists who used to go painting together. It was one of Mum and Dad's wedding presents. Seeing it on the floor instead of on the wall where it should have been was pretty shocking, almost enough to make me feel sick again.

I was slowly starting to work out what was happening when I looked up and saw an antelope staring me in the face. Actually, it was only a stuffed antelope head, from one of Dad's hunting trips. I looked a bit further up, and there was Dad, smiling, holding the head in his arms. Dad's head was right between the antlers.

– Howdy, Prof, Dad said.

He calls me Prof because I get good marks in school.

– Hi, I said.

– Well, the time has come. Get packin'.

I looked back into the antelope's face. It had a little smile, like it was making fun of me. Dad stepped around me and stuffed the head into a wooden crate. I looked out the living room window. On the street in front of our house was a U-Haul trailer hitched to our station wagon. I could also see the back of the Melton Realty sign on our front lawn. I figured it out then, all right. We were moving.

Anybody who's read this far, I bet, will say 'Yeah, right. The guy's family is moving, and everybody else knows, but somehow he doesn't. Next, please.' Well, I don't know what to say, except I swear I really did forget, that is, if I ever really even knew in the first place. Mr Baldwin talked once about how people can go from day to day not seeing what's right in front of them, just to make their life easier. He was talking about politics, but I guess he could have been talking about me.

About three months ago, Mum and Dad started saying the house was getting too small. What they really meant was that we were getting bigger. There was always a line-up for the bathroom in the morning (which I didn't notice much because I was always the last one up), and the girls especially were taking forever in there, doing whatever girls do in the can. Even I got locked out sometimes, but it was no big deal to me. I could always take a leak into the hole in the utility room floor. But I guess Mum and Dad figured we couldn't all do that. They made up their mind that we needed a house with two bathrooms. Also, as we got bigger it got tougher to share bedrooms. We always seemed to be bumping into each other, or getting into fights when people left their gaunch lying around, or snored, or cracked their knuckles, or had smelly feet, or wanted to hang up a poster nobody else liked. You should have seen Susan and Anne when Mary put up Donny Osmond. If we had more rooms, Mum and Dad thought, maybe those fights would stop.

The first time I saw the For Sale sign on the lawn, about a month before, I asked what was going on. Dad said we were testing the market. That meant seeing how much our house was worth. If I'd been smart I would have figured out that the next thing you do after that is sell your house. I didn't figure it out, though. Maybe I didn't want to. Maybe when you've only ever known one house and one neighbourhood, the idea of leaving it is too much for your brain to take. And because I always came home the back way, it was easy to forget about that sign in the front yard. I couldn't forget about it any more, though. No way.

People were still zigzagging around with boxes as I stood there in the middle of the living room. Nobody seemed sad about leaving at all. Duncan and Richard were competing to see who could stuff papers the fastest. Howard was helping Dad with the heaviest stuff. The girls were all putting girl stuff from their dressers into green garbage bags. Susan kept singing that Canned Heat song, 'On the Road Again'. They were at Woodstock. Sam was lying in the corner looking depressed, just like he was at lunchtime. I guess he knew even then.

I did what I usually do when I don't like what's going on at home. I took off for my bedroom, upstairs at the end of the hall. I didn't make it all the way, though. Mum was just coming out of her room with some boxes in her hands, and we bumped into each other.

– Whooah, Rip! she said.

– Sorry, I said.

– If I'd known you were coming, I'd have baked a cake.

Mum says that whenever I'm late for something. It's another line from one of those weird old songs she knows. I have no idea what she means by it.

– A little late, aren't we? she asked.

– Pretty late, yeah.

– Some kind of after-school sports thing?

– Yeah.

Grade fours don't even have after-school sports things, but it sure beat telling her about Sister and Tommy and Jesus Alou. She'd find out soon enough about that stuff anyway, I thought.

– Well, now that you're here, you'd better hop to it, Mum said.

I didn't answer. Mum always knows when I'm not happy.

– Want to talk? she asked.

– Yeah.

We went into her and Dad's bedroom. I hardly ever used to go in there. It always felt like breaking into someone else's house or something. There was all this adult stuff in it. Dad kept his hunting ammunition in one of the closets, and had a habit of leaving his dentures in a glass of water by the side of the bed. One time I knocked it over by accident, and sent the dentures flying all the way across the room. There'd also be stuff of Mum's like funny-looking girdles and wigs and things. Sometimes I'd use the Styrofoam wig dummy for boxing practice. I'd be Muhammad Ali and the dummy, which looked like Audrey Hepburn, would be Joe Frazier. It has dents and scratches all over it now. Anyway, today there was stuff spread all over the big bed, mostly old hats and jackets of Mum's that she never wears any more. They're like something a movie star from the forties would wear. Mum says she keeps them for sentimental reasons. We moved some of them and sat down on the bed.

– So, Mum said, are you as excited as everyone else? You don't look it right now.

– No, I said. I'm not.

My bottom lip was shaking, like it does before you cry.

– That's all right, you know, Mum said. It's natural to feel sad, leaving all your ...

– That's not why I'm not excited! I said. I didn't even know we were moving!

– You didn't *know*?

– Yeah. I mean, no. Maybe I forgot. I don't know. But I didn't expect all this. I thought we were going to hollow out pumpkins or something. Not *move*. Why didn't you tell me?

– But I ... oh, goodness. Lordy love a duck. You didn't know?

I looked at Mum. She looked like a ghost.

– That's incredible, she said. How could you not have known? We've been talking about it since ...

She stopped and stared at me. She was probably remembering other times when I haven't known what was going on, like vacations, or somebody like the parish priest coming over. I'm always the last one to know, if I know at all. It's not that I don't want to know stuff. It's just that I'm always off someplace with a book or a CHED Chart or watching a game or playing 45s. People are always thinking they've told me stuff when they haven't. It's not their fault. I don't blame them or anything. Still, moving was a pretty big thing not to know. But like I said, maybe they did tell me, and I just didn't want to know. I don't know.

– Where are we going, anyway? I asked.

– To that nice house in Londonderry. You remember. The one with the shag carpeting. We saw it a few weeks ago.

– Oh, yeah.

I remembered that one because that was the only one of the house-viewing trips I went on. You go to these places and a real estate person tries to tell you how great they are. This house had more bedrooms than ours, and a garage, and a bigger back yard. It was right up the street from where they were building some new mall that was supposed to be the biggest in the world or something. How exciting.

What really got everybody dancing for joy, though, was the shag carpeting. It was everywhere, all through the living and dining rooms, up the stairs and in the hall and bedrooms. I was surprised it wasn't in the bathtub. If you've never seen shag, it's about two inches deep. It's supposed to look like grass, I think, but it reminds me more of those weird tentacle plants you see on *The Undersea World of Jacques Cousteau*, grabbing fish on the bottom of the ocean. The real estate lady demonstrated how you rake the rug, and everybody oohed and aahed. Nobody seemed to stop and think that you have to rake it *and* vacuum it. That's twice as much work as a regular carpet. Another thing about shag is that when you walk on it in your sock feet, you get totally filled with static electricity, and the next time you touch something metal, like a doorknob, you get a huge shock, and send sparks flying all over. It's got to be the stupidest invention of all time, and we were moving to a house full of it.

– I hate that place, I said.

– Oh, come now, Mum said. It'll grow on you. What about the big new mall?

– What's wrong with Northgate?

– This one will be bigger, with more shops. Something like a hundred, they say.

– Big deal. I only use two shops at Northgate anyway.

That was true. They were Scotty's Records and Tapes, and the Nut House, for candy and malts. What could you do with another ninety-eight, anyway? What would they sell?

– When are we going? I asked.

– Umm, well … that's another thing we thought you knew. We leave tomorrow morning, bright and early.

– *Tomorrow?*

– Yes. The new owners are moving in at noon. We need to be

gone by then. This must seem awfully sudden, but we just got word last week.

– So that means, like, tonight is our last night in this house?

It was a pretty stupid question. So much stuff was already packed, we'd be lucky to have beds to sleep on.

– I'm afraid so, Mum said.

– So, I guess I'll have further to go to school now, eh? I asked. Mum got the ghost look again.

– Oh, my goodness, she said.

– What do you mean? I asked.

I knew it wouldn't be good.

– Well, she said, you won't be going to St. Paul's any more. You've got a new school now, Father Leo Green, up on 144th Avenue. They've just finished building it. You know, I'm surprised there wasn't some sort of announcement.

– What are you talking about?

– In your class, I mean. About the fact that it was your last day. Mary had a nice little send-off, apparently.

Little light bulbs were going on in my head. I remembered Monsieur Houle, the French teacher, wishing me good luck after class. He must have known. But why didn't the other teachers say anything? Mr Baldwin's a sub, so he might not have known, and Mrs Horn, well, I've told you about her. That only left Mr Newcombe, the gym teacher, who didn't really know I existed anyway, and Sister Arlene. Maybe, I thought, she was so hot and bothered about the Jesus Alou thing that she forgot to say goodbye. But then it came back to me that I'd missed the last ten minutes, which is when she probably would have said something. What went on in those last ten minutes, anyway?

I must have looked pretty stunned. This was a lot to take in. Mum put her arm around my shoulder.

– Chin up there, Rip. Londonderry's only thirty blocks away. Just up 137th, past the big Ukrainian graveyard.

Thirty blocks! That might as well have been in the Yukon. All my friends lived close enough that we could practically shout from our back yards and hear each other. It was different enough just going to Tommy's today.

I didn't say anything to Mum. I wasn't trying to be rude. I just couldn't make any words come out of my mouth. Mum stood up.

– Supper's on downstairs. Let's skedaddle, she said.

We skedaddled down. The chairs were already packed, so people were sitting wherever they could, on boxes or the phone book or even the floor. It was like being in a bomb shelter or something. It was also weird to be all together at one time like that for supper. Usually, even on days when we're all home, we'll just take off with our plates to different parts of the house. Now, with all of us there, and the walls all empty, everything was all loud and echoey. Everybody was yakking all at once, and Mary was marching around singing one of those annoying Shirley Temple songs she always sings. I couldn't really hear what anybody was saying, so I just sat over by Sam, concentrating on my pork, beets, and apple sauce. When we were all done eating, Dad came up to me.

– What do you say we take a break and watch some ball, Prof? he asked.

– Yeah! I said.

With everything that was going on, I'd kind of forgotten about the game tonight, the first ever World Series night game. Me and Dad went downstairs and turned the TV on just as the national anthem was ending. It was nice to be in the basement, away from all the the noise and weirdness upstairs, and to be watching baseball, which always gets me excited and relaxed at the same time. We settled onto the couch, which was still there. As they did the pregame stuff, talking about the starting pitchers and things, we chatted a bit.

– So, Dad said, your mother tells me you're not too keen on this moving thing.

– It'll grow on me, I said.

That was about the last thing I meant. It wasn't how I felt at all. But I don't really like getting into arguments with Dad.

– Sure it will, he said. Besides, I hear those Londonderry girls are really something. You'll be fighting them off.

He knows I hate it when he talks about girls like that.

– Yeah, I sure will, I said.

Two interesting things happened early in the game. One was that the Pirates starter injured his arm or something, and they had to bring in this rookie relief pitcher, Bruce Kison, who looked like a giant grasshopper. Everybody thought he'd get destroyed, but that's not what happened at all. What Kison did was scare the wits out of the hitters. Every second or third guy, he'd nearly kill with a high inside pitch. He even beaned a couple and put them on base. But the other hitters, instead of driving them in, would be so scared of being beaned that they'd strike out. Here was this rookie, with no control, beating the world champs. It was wild.

The other cool thing happened on Clemente's second at bat. He got a hanging curve out over the plate, and drove it out toward right field. It looked like a sure homer if it stayed fair. It ended up hitting the foul pole, two decks up, and landing back on the field. Clemente went into his home run trot, and the fans and me and Dad went crazy, until we noticed that the right field ump was calling the ball foul. That was nuts, because you could tell from the bounce that it had to be fair. Clemente and Danny Murtaugh, the Pirates manager, went hog wild, screaming in the ump's face, but he didn't change his mind. They never do. Clemente had to go back to the plate. Now, most hitters would be so cheesed at losing a home run that they'd just sulk and strike out, but Clemente, on the very next pitch, hit it in the exact same direction, only lower. This one hit the top of the outfield fence, and Clemente pulled into second with a double. There was a great close-up of him standing there, with his hands on his hips, glaring out at the ump with a 'Take that!' look on his face. Dad and me turned to each other and, at exactly the same time, nodded. It was great.

– Got his card yet? Dad asked.

– No, I said.

Maybe it was the card question that reminded me, because right then I thought of Keith. He was supposed to come over and watch the game with me. Maybe Freddy too. I'd forgotten all about it. What was really weird was that Keith hadn't just come over, or at least phoned to say he couldn't. The next inning break, I went upstairs to call him, to see what was going on.

When I got to the kitchen and went to pick up the phone, something made me freeze in my tracks. I stopped and looked around. The change just in the last half hour was unbelievable. All the boxes and cartons and piles of crumpled-up paper were gone. Every one of them. I checked the fridge, and all that was in there were one bottle of milk and some leftover porridge.

136

Tomorrow's breakfast, I guessed.

Looking into that almost bare fridge, it really, completely hit me that we were leaving and wouldn't be coming back. It was one thing to see furniture and books and records getting packed, but when a place has almost no food in it, that's a different kind of empty. I realized right then that everything I did tonight and tomorrow morning would be for the last time in this house.

When I tried to think ahead one night, to sleeping in a different bed (well, actually the same bed) in a different house, it didn't work. My brain just wouldn't do it. There was just a blank. It was a pretty scary feeling. I thought of those old pictures, from when they thought the earth was flat, of sailors going over the edge, and falling off into nothing.

The house was pretty quiet by this time. Susan, Howard, Ann and Duncan were all out, probably at goodbye parties or something. Richard had a lacrosse practice. Mary was sitting on the stairs singing this song about animal crackers that she heard in a Shirley Temple movie. She sings it all the time. I hate it.

Standing there in the kitchen, I did this experiment I do sometimes. It's kind of fun. What you do is try to empty your head of everything that's in it at that minute. Once all that stuff is gone, you listen really close to hear what song is playing in your head. There's always something playing, at least in *my* head. Sometimes I do the experiment just for fun, but other times I'll do it if I'm nervous or mad about something. Once, when the Leafs missed the playoffs and it seemed like the end of the world, I listened for a song, and it was that one by the Rolling Stones, 'Jumpin' Jack Flash', where the singer keeps going 'It's all right now'. It made me feel better, even though it's a pretty creepy song. So I emptied my head there in the kitchen, and listened hard, and the song that came up was 'Homeward Bound', by Simon and Garfunkel. Great, I thought. Here I am leaving home and my brain's giving me a song about going back home. Thanks a lot. I don't know what makes a song come. Maybe this time it was just the word home. I stopped the experiment.

NINETEEN

Being in that empty, echoey house wasn't much fun, so I figured I'd put down the phone and go out on the back step for a while. It was kind of nice to get some fresh air and look at the back yard, which wasn't changed at all. It's not like we were going to rip out all the trees and plants when we left.

Not far from where I sat was my Centennial tree. In 1967, they gave every Canadian kindergarten kid a box of dirt with a tiny tree in it, and told us that in a hundred years, on Canada's two-hundredth birthday, they'd be a hundred feet tall. Mine was about the same height as me now, which is about four feet six.

For the middle of October, it was a pretty nice night. I sat there concentrating on sounds one by one. There was a lawn mower coming from a couple of blocks away, and the old couple next door, who I've barely seen in my life, were talking in German. Some birds, robins I think, were hanging out on the telephone wires, singing. Our science teacher told us that birds only sing when they're mad or scared, but these birds sounded pretty happy to me. Maybe they were fighting over a worm or something.

There was another sound, too, that I didn't notice at first. It was music. Sometimes it's hard to tell if the music you're hearing is in your own head or somewhere else, which was maybe why I didn't hear this music at first, or think about where it was coming from. I might have just thought it was in my head. The closer I listened, though, the more I knew that somebody somewhere was playing it. It was nothing I knew, and it wasn't the kind of stuff you hear on the radio. It was hard to make out through the lawn mowers and birds and stuff, but I was pretty sure I heard an accordion, and a violin, and one of those weird little guitars, like a mandolin.

The other thing I heard was Mum and Dad's voices coming from inside. I didn't pay any attention at first, but then I realized they were arguing. That doesn't happen much. Sometimes Mum gets mad about stuff, like when Dad invites a bunch of his hunting buddies over without telling her first, or the time we kept this bear in our basement. It was this cub black bear that they were moving to a zoo, but there was some problem, so Dad said we could keep it for a day in a cage in our basement, but the day turned into two weeks. We all thought it was great having a bear in the house, but Mum wasn't too thrilled because it was stinking up the place and she was the one who had to clean the straw and stuff from around the cage. Anyway, because it was so unusual to hear them arguing, I started to listen.

– It's unbelievable, Dad said.

– But he says he wasn't told, Mum said.

– Wasn't *told?* Wasn't bloody listening, more likely. Damnation, what else have we all been talking about? Besides, you'd think he might have figured it out for himself. The boy is ten years old.

– Nine.

– Nine, ten, so what? Why didn't you make it clear to him?

– *Me?* Why is it always *my* responsibility? All this was your idea to begin with. I've said all along that all we had to do was add another bathroom in the basement. There was never any need to ...

– Lord! Can't I have some peace? Do you have to shout it out from the mountaintop for all the street to hear?

– *I'm* shouting? *Who's* shouting?

I had three choices. I could keep sitting there hearing them, I could try sneaking past them into the basement to keep watching the game, or I could go for a walk. I picked the last one. It seemed like the best idea. Besides, I was really curious about that music off in the distance. It seemed to be coming from over in the direction of the school, so I stood up and walked closer to the alley to hear it better. I was starting to like it more and more, so I figured I'd try to find out who was playing it. Mum and Dad were so busy they probably wouldn't even notice I was gone.

Finding where music is coming from isn't as easy as you might think. It's not like seeing smoke from a fire, where you can just run over and see what's going on. Music is invisible. It's sort of in the air, not floating like a balloon really, more kind of spreading in every direction, like gas. It also gets louder or softer depending on the wind. Just a little breeze can change the way it sounds. So I was having a pretty hard time finding it. I took the path past the Pippigs' place, and it got louder, but when I turned right toward 132nd, I started to lose it again. I must have looked like an idiot, standing there on the sidewalk, shuffling this way and that to test which way the music was loudest. I even tried shutting my eyes and following it that way, but I bumped into a parked car and gave up that idea.

Then, all of a sudden, I could hear the music really clearly. The breeze must have been blowing just the right way. I followed the sound. Now I could hear not just the instruments, but the sound of people clapping and voices laughing. Getting closer, I could also smell something like a barbecue. There was definitely a party going on. I thought it would be neat to get real close, and sit and listen to the music for a while. It was sounding better all the time.

The music pulled me into the alleyway of the row-housing where most of my friends live. I went past the giant split-level birdhouse, and the yard with four little plastic swimming pools, and waved to the guy who's always working on World War II motorcycles. The music made me feel like I was in one of those foreign movies they're always showing on *Stardust Theatre*. Kids in those are always carrying long loaves of French bread, and when they talk the sound doesn't match the way their lips are moving.

About two houses away from where the music was coming from, I finally realized what I probably should have known all along. It was the Santuccis' place I was heading to. The voices were all in Italian, and some of them, like Mr Santucci's, were familiar. So now I had two choices. I could turn right around, to make sure I didn't get beat up, or I could keep going. I kept going. The music sort of had me hypnotized.

I got to the Santuccis' back fence, and peeked in through a hole. The first thing that caught my eye was this giant dead pig on a stick, getting spun around over a fire. I didn't know pigs got that big. The guy spinning the stick was this chubby little guy, wearing a chef's hat and an apron over a regular suit. Strung around the yard they had a bunch of those patio lanterns, all different colours. Little kids were tearing around everywhere, around the pig and between people's legs. There were a bunch of teenagers, too. Some of the boys I recognized. They were those guys from Little Italy who used to grab me and force me to be the goalie when they played road hockey. I looked at the girls, who were all standing in the far side of the yard from the guys. They were all really good-looking, wearing these sort of old-fashioned party dresses. They all had long dark hair in fancy hairdos, and dark eyes, and dark skin that made their teeth look really white when they smiled. Every now and then, one of the boys would shout something in Italian from across the yard, and they'd all giggle and blush like mad. I was getting crushes on them, just sitting there peeking. It was weird.

Over in one corner, near the back door, I finally saw who was making the music. It was these three tiny little old guys in black suits and hats. I'm pretty sure I've seen them before, at Borden Park. On weekends there you see huge gangs of these old guys, sitting around picnic tables, playing chess and smoking these funny little cigarettes. Even on the hottest days, when everybody else is running around in shorts, these guys have their black suits on, with the shirts buttoned all the way up. None of them looks more than five feet tall. So there were three of them, playing this great music, sort of sad but dancy too. Adults were standing around them, some chatting all happily and some looking a bit sad. Mr Santucci was half walking and half dancing around, singing opera stuff that didn't really go with what the little guys were playing. Under one arm he had this gigantic hunk of cheese, shaped like a hockey puck. In the other hand he had a little knife. He'd skip up to people, cut off a slice of cheese, and feed it to them, whether they wanted it or not. He was totally happy. It was hard to believe he was the same guy who looked ready to tear my head off at lunchtime in the grocery store.

I got so caught up watching everything that I guess I got a bit careless. What I forgot was that the sun was setting right behind me, so every time I put my head by the fence hole I made a big shadow, and when I moved it away, the sun would come shining back in. That must have been how Tony Santucci saw me. He saw a shadow go over him, looked up, and there was my face in the hole. I didn't move in time. Tony's eyebrows went up, he shouted something in Italian, and went running to the back gate. I got up, took a step backwards, and got my pants stuck in a thorn bush. I ripped the pantleg off the bush, but it slowed me down. I didn't stand a chance of getting away from Tony. I ran, but it wasn't long before I felt his breath and saw his hand on my shoulder. There was no use trying to escape. He had me.

– Hey, little guy, where you goin' so fast? I been lookin' for you, he said.

I thought my only hope might be to try and explain why I squealed on his little brother, and I didn't seem to have much time, so I tried.

– I'm sorry, I said. I didn't mean it. I meant to squeal on ...

– Save the speech, Mr Longhair, Tony said. I'm takin' you to see my papa. He's got somethin' to say to you.

Great, I thought. I'll get chewed out again, then beat up. I was starting to wish I could trade places with that giant pig.

He kept his hand on my shoulder and led me back to the party. All the while, he was whistling along with the accordion music. Only the meanest guys can whistle just before they beat somebody up.

– Beautiful night we're havin', huh? he said. Perfect for a party.

– Yeah, I said.

Perfect for having your clock cleaned, too.

We turned into the yard. The party was in full gear. Voices were getting louder, the music was getting faster, the pig was getting browner. The chubby chef was painting it with some kind of food polish. Nobody paid much attention to Tony escorting me into the yard, even though I really stood out. Nobody else there had blond hair, and nobody else was shaking with fear. Mr Santucci was still prancing around giving cheese slices to everybody, until he saw me from across the yard. He stopped right in his tracks, stared for a minute, and put the cheese and knife down on a tray. He walked up to me slowly and crouched down so his face was level with mine. Here we go, I thought.

– Yup, you the guy, he said.

Get it over with. Just get it over with.

– Come over here, he said. I got a somethin' to show you.

He got up and walked over by the fire. I followed

– Look at this, little fella, he said, pointing at something.

I couldn't figure out what he meant at first. All I could see was a pile of twigs, like you'd use for a marshmallow roast or something. The chef guy picked up a few and stuck them in the fire. I was about to ask Mr Santucci what I was supposed to be

looking at, when something caught my eye. It was the tip of one
of the twigs. You could tell it hadn't just been snapped off,
because it was cut straight through, all smooth. It was the kind of
mark you'd make with a sharp knife. Or an axe. Mr Santucci
crouched down to my face again.

– I gotta apologize to you, he said.

His breath was like cheese and wine, and he had one hand
over his heart. It looked like he was about to propose to me or
something. I just stood and waited for him to go on.

– You see these sticks? he asked.

– Yeah, I said.

– Well, can you guess who cut 'em?

Of course. Little twigs, cut with an axe, by a little guy. I could
feel my heart pounding.

– Giuseppe? I asked.

– You got it, Mr Santucci said. My little bambino tryin' to be a
big man. He musta heard us talkin' about sticks for the roast, so
he went out and chopped a few. Did a pretty good job, too, if I say
so.

He chuckled and I chuckled along because it seemed like a
good idea to. Then his face went serious again.

– But that's not the point, if he did a good job or not, he said.
He shouldn't a done it. We can't have little guys runnin' around
choppin' stuff. I gotta be more careful where I leave my axe.

– Yeah, I said.

I was a little less scared by now. Mr Santucci went on.

– And you, my little friend, did a the right thing. I should a
been thankin' you, not scarin' you to death. That's why I wanted
Tony to find you. As a man of honour, it's my duty to offer you,
on behalf of all the Santuccis, my deepest and most a humble
apologies.

He put his hand on his heart again, and went down on one
knee. It was a bit embarrassing. I saw one of the good-looking
girls giggling and pointing at us.

– That's okay, I said.

Mr Santucci took me by the shoulders, shook me a bit, and
kissed me once on each cheek. His face felt all sweaty and
whiskery.

– Spoken like a true gentleman, he said.

He stood up and ruffled my hair. A few people cheered.

– And so, he said, allow me to invite a you to join in this feast, in a honour of the engagement of my daughter Alma. She's goin' back to the old country to join a fine young man. My heart aches, but I'm filled with joy. That's a life.

I looked over at Alma. She's my sister Susan's age. She used to go to O'Connor but she quit to be a secretary for a trucking company. A bunch of old ladies were standing around her, crying and making the sign of the cross with Giuseppe and some of his tiny friends playing hide-and-seek around them. When I looked back at Mr Santucci, he was holding the cheese and knife again.

– Permit a me the privilege, he said, of sharin' my provolone with a you.

He held out a piece on the edge of the knife. I took it and popped it in my mouth. It was pretty good. Then he started dancing around the yard again, singing and feeding people.

So there I was in the middle of this party. I wasn't going to get beat up. Not only that, but it looked like I could even have some fun if I wanted. Nobody was staring or treating me weird or anything. They acted like it was natural for me to be there. The only thing was that everybody, even people like Tony who I know knows English, was talking in Italian. I guess they do that when they're all relaxed or excited. So I strolled around the yard for a while, trying to figure out what people were talking about. Some of the men and teenage guys were in a big argument about soccer. They call it football. One man was standing with his arms folded, shaking his head, saying 'Pele! Pele!' over and over, while the other twenty or so guys shouted the names of Italian players, and other stuff that sounded like insults. The old ladies were talking about Alma. They kept looking over at her and saying words like 'bella'. I didn't really think she was as bella as most of the girls there.

After a few minutes of wandering around getting winked at and being told stuff I didn't understand, I was backing up and bumped into a table. I turned around, and it was covered with about five hundred paper cups full of drinks. Mrs Santucci was just finishing putting them down when she saw me standing there.

– Feelin' a thirsty? she asked.

– Kind of, I said.

Actually, I was dying of thirst.

– Wella, helpa yourself, she said. We got a pop, we got a Kool-Aid, we got a vino. Whatever you want.

Then she walked away. But there was a problem. All the drinks were pretty much the same red colour. There was no way to tell the pop from the Kool-Aid from the wine. I watched to see what other people were taking, but they seemed to be just grabbing anything. So I picked up the nearest cup. It was pretty small, so I just drank it all in one gulp. It was only after I swallowed that I realized it was wine. I thought I was going to faint for a minute, but I got steady again, and then I started to feel kind of neat, like you do in the middle of a yawn or a sneeze. Still, I was a bit worried about getting drunk, so I figured I'd have a pop or Kool-Aid to balance out the wine. I picked up another cup, and I don't know, I guess I wasn't thinking, because instead of trying to sip it or sniff it to find out what it was, I just drained it like the first one. It turned out that this one was wine, too.

The next few minutes aren't very clear in my mind. I remember the lights from the patio lanterns looking like they were swirling. I'm pretty sure I walked beside Mr Santucci for a while, singing opera stuff with him. I think I gave some drinks to the little musician guys, and talked a bit with the giant roasting pig. It wasn't just me getting weirder either, I don't think. The whole party seemed to be picking up speed. Some space was cleared on the patio and a couple started dancing this really cool dance where they held their hands on their hips and kind of tiptoed around each other. I might have tried to join them, but it was too hard to get tiptoed in my Hush Puppies. I stood and watched with other people, clapping along with the music and shouting stuff I hoped sounded Italian.

Even clapping and shouting were hard to concentrate on after the two wines, though, so after a minute I gave up and wandered some more. The chef and two other guys were starting to carve slices off the pig, who was still on the stick with a giant smile frozen on his face. I backed off from that and started, without thinking about it, to dance around by myself. It wasn't the tiptoed dance, though. It was just something I made up as I went along, sort of part ballet dance and partly that go-go dancing, like bikini girls do on *Laugh-In*. Lots of people were dancing by this time, so I had to try not to bump into them, which was hard after the wines. One old guy who was waltzing around with his wife elbowed me in the head without meaning to, and I stumbled backwards off the patio and onto the lawn. That's when something really neat happened.

I stopped stumbling by bumping into something soft and white. To pull myself up, I grabbed onto the white thing. It looked like a curtain. But then I felt two hands grab me by the armpits, lift me up, and toss me in the air. For a second I was flying above the coloured lanterns, and when I landed, it was into the soft white thing again. The thing was a dress, and a girl was inside it. She laughed, said something in Italian, and put me down. I was pretty dizzy, and whichever way I looked, I saw white. When I turned my head up to the sky, I saw five or six faces smiling down at me, and what looked like miles of black hair hanging down and tickling my face. I was surrounded by all these gorgeous teenage Italian girls. Oh boy.

The next thing I knew, they were taking turns grabbing me and tossing me up and down. I didn't exactly struggle to resist. The best part was landing. These bare arms would grab me around the waist, and then I'd get pulled right up close, until I was face to face with a beautiful, dark-eyed, wild-haired perfumey girl, who'd pinch my cheek and hand me on to the next one. When they got tired of tossing me up, they let me lie on my back on the grass. I thought they were giving me a breather, but then I noticed they were whispering to each other, and all of a sudden they bent down and started tickling me all at once, covering my face with their hair and calling me Italian names. I laughed my head off, pretending to fight them off, squirming and kicking my legs. They laughed just as hard. Finally, just when I thought I'd get sick from the wine and from laughing too hard, they seemed to tire themselves out. They stopped tickling one by one, stood up, and pulled me up with them. A couple of them messed my hair and pulled my cheeks again. It was the most fun I've ever had in my life.

A little thought at the back of my head bugged me a bit, though, and it kept growing. I was missing the game on TV. Not only that, but I'd just taken off without telling anybody, and gone to a party and drunk wine and gotten thrown around by girls. It was probably a good idea to go back, to keep from getting bawled out too bad and to catch the rest of the game. It must have been the fifth or sixth inning already.

I couldn't very well just leave the party without saying goodbye. That wouldn't have been polite. So I went around to different people, teenage girls and Tony and old ladies and even tiny little Giuseppe, saying stuff like 'Well, see ya' and 'Gotta go now', but I couldn't get anyone's attention. Finally, I found Mr Santucci.

– Thanks for the party, I said. I'm going now.

He didn't look at me, just kept gabbing with some old guys, so I tapped him, pretty hard actually, on the side of the leg. He looked down all squinty at me.

– Well, see ya, I said.

It took some time, but Mr Santucci bent down, and looked right into my face. He seemed to be having a hard time focusing on me. In a minute, he started to smile.

– Yup, he said. You the guy.

– Pardon me? I asked.

– You the guy, he said. I gotta apologize to you. Giuseppe never shoulda had that axe. You did the right thing.

He went to grab my cheeks, but he forgot about the cup and fork he was holding. Some wine from the cup splashed onto my shirt, and the fork almost stabbed me in the ear. He didn't notice.

– On a behalf of all the Santuccis, let me extend a my deepest …

I backed away from him, really carefully so the fork wouldn't scrape my face.

– Well, thanks again, I said, walking backwards. So long.

Before I knew it, I was backed right out of the yard and into the alley. It was dark out, so the only light came from the patio lanterns. I made my way in the red and yellow and green light out to the street, then turned to go home. But something felt wrong. I was going home to watch the rest of the game, but all along I was supposed to watch it with Keith. I felt bad about forgetting about him like that, and I wasn't exactly thrilled about going back home right then, so I turned and headed for the Puzniaks' place.

TWENTY

The music got quieter as I walked away, until by the time I got to the Puzniaks' back yard, you never would have guessed a party was going on anywhere. I went up their back sidewalk, past the toolshed where me and Keith used to pretend we were the man in the iron mask locked up in the Tower of London. We'd stick pails on our heads. The wine and getting thrown around was still making it a bit hard for me to move straight. I rang the doorbell, probably more times than I had to.

I'm not sure how long I stood there waiting, but it must have been a while, because I had time to think about lots of stuff. It was a weird mix of good and bad. I'd get worried about being in trouble with Sister Arlene, until I remembered that I wouldn't even be going back to her class. That would relax me until I remembered that the reason I wouldn't be going back was because I was moving. That got me down until I thought about those Italian girls. I was in the middle of a daydream about getting tickled when the back door finally opened. It was Keith.

– You're missing the game, Keith said.

As usual, no hi or anything. Not even a smile.

– Uh, yeah, I said. I figured I'd come over and watch the rest of it with you.

– What's that on your shirt? he asked.

– What's what? I asked.

– All that red stuff.

I looked down. In the back porch light, it looked pretty bad, like, well, blood.

– That's pop, I said.

– Pop?

– Yeah. Tahiti Treat. I got all excited watching the game and spilled it on myself.

– Oh.

He still just stood there, sticking his head out the door and staring at my shirt.

– Can I come in? I asked.

– Come in? Oh, yeah, sure, come on in.

I went behind Keith into the little landing between the basement stairs and the kitchen. I thought we'd go straight into the living room, but instead he turned in the other direction, through the kitchen, to go upstairs.

– Wait here by the door, he said. I've got to go get my satchel.

Keith's got this little shoulder bag he likes to carry around, even when there's nothing in it. It always used to be just his bag, until we watched *Tom Sawyer* on the after-school special, and learned the word satchel. Now, if you call it anything else, he gets all mad.

I waited by the door like Keith told me to. From where I was, you could see through the kitchen, and into a little sliver of the living room through a sliding door. The baseball game was on pretty loud, but just as they were about to say the score, the volume went down all the way. The set was still on, though. You could tell by the way the light danced around on the wall. I started to wonder about stuff, like why would someone turn down the volume but keep watching? And why was Keith upstairs getting his satchel when we were supposed to be watching the game? I thought I'd at least take a look to see the score, so I crossed the kitchen and peeked in to see the TV.

Right away I could tell I should have stayed where Keith said. His baba, in her big black dress and her head kerchief thing, holding a walking stick in one hand, was bending over fiddling with the controls on the TV. She'd managed to turn it down, but she couldn't figure out how to turn it off. The TV had the kind of buttons you're supposed to spin like a dial, but she kept trying to push and pull them. By mistake she turned the volume back up, even louder than it was before, and finally gave up and stood up straight, which was hard for her to do.

Even though the feeling that something was wrong kept getting stronger, I didn't go back to the back door. It was hard to take my eyes off Keith's baba, and I was also still sort of trying to see around her to find out how the game was going. She started to turn around, stepping about an inch at a time, with the TV blaring away behind her. I heard something about Milt May hitting a double, then looked up and saw that Keith's baba was looking right at me.

149

The thing to do right then would have been to say 'Pardon me' and go back to waiting in the landing. But Keith's baba's eyes wouldn't let me move. Slowly, she turned her head to look over at the couch on the other side of the room, and I did too. It was like I had no choice.

What we both looked at was Mr Puzniak. He was sort of half on and half off the couch, wearing an undershirt and a pair of Disneyland boxer shorts, both not very clean. His face was all whiskery, like my dad's after a hunting trip, and his gut looked a lot bigger than it did the last time I saw him. Under the sound of the shouting baseball announcer you could just barely hear Mr Puzniak snoring. I thought it was weird that a guy would fall asleep in the middle of a World Series game, especially with the sound up full blast. Then I looked a bit closer. The arm that was hanging off the couch was still holding an empty wine bottle. Three or four other bottles, some standing up and some lying sideways, were on the floor in front of the couch. Cigarette butts were everywhere, overflowing from an ashtray and butted into bottles. For a second his snoring stopped, and I thought he might be dead, but then it started up again.

Keith's baba and me looked back at each other. She started to shuffle in my direction. With her free hand she signalled for me to go into the kitchen. I did, and in a minute she was in there with me. There was a chair in the middle of the floor that must have been her favourite, because she headed straight for it, settled into it real slow, and put her stick across her lap. I stood there with my back to the door while she leaned forward, looking at me like she was about to start telling a story. She never did start, though, just sat there looking at me, sometimes squinting at me like I was a mile away, and sometimes just giving me a blank stare. I just shuffled. I wondered what could be taking Keith so long. The TV kept blasting from the living room, the light kept dancing on the wall through the sliding door. I heard a bottle fall over and roll around on the floor a bit. All this time, I was looking back at Keith's baba.

It was the first time I'd really seen her up close. She had these amazing warts on her chin and cheeks, and a moustache bigger than the one Tony Santucci was always trying to grow. Her hands looked strong enough to tear you apart. They were all sort of twisted and brown, like a tree root. They looked like part of the walking stick she was holding. Her dress was pretty long, and she seemed to have a few layers of sweaters and skirts and stuff under it, plus one of those button-up sweaters over it. You could just see her ankles and the top of her feet, all swelled up and veiny, looking like they were going to burst out of these little slipper things she was wearing.

As Keith's baba and me kept looking at each other, I thought about how this situation was kind of the opposite of *The Time Tunnel*, when those two dorks in their turtlenecks go back in history. Keith's baba looked like somebody had just zapped her from the past into now. But the funny thing was, I felt like *I* was the one in the wrong place, like *she* was normal but everything around her was weird and wrong. She looked like she was always the same and always would be the same. It was all this other stuff, like being in a row house in Edmonton with a strange loud machine blaring, and her son-in-law snoring in his gaunch in the next room and a kid in a red-stained shirt looking at her, that was weird. I thought about all the stuff she must have done in her life, like leaving the place where she was born, living in a hole in the ground, working on a farm bending over to plant and pick stuff all the time. I bet of all those things, this situation right now felt the weirdest to her. Maybe she guessed what I was thinking, because she gave me this little smile and nodded, the kind of nod people give you when they're saying they understand. It gave me goosebumps.

Time was doing weird things. It seemed like forever that I was waiting for Keith to come back down with his satchel, but I saw by the clock on the wall that it was only about five minutes later when he came into the kitchen. He looked at me and his baba, then put his hand on her shoulder and said something in Ukrainian. It must have meant something like 'I'm going out for a while', because she just nodded and smiled again, and me and Keith went out the back door.

I didn't ask Keith why we weren't staying to watch the game. It would have been a pretty stupid question. I just assumed we were going to watch the end at my place, so I was surprised when we got to the sidewalk and he turned the other way, in the direction of 132nd.

– Hey, I said. Where are you going?

– What do you mean?

– I mean, let's go to my place. Don't you want to watch the end of the game?

He kept walking the other way, going pretty slow.

– I think I'll just walk around, he said.

He didn't ask if I wanted to walk with him, but I started to anyway. It would have been rude just to turn around and go home. Anyway, it was a really nice night for the middle of October. We both weren't wearing jackets, but we weren't even cold. I caught up with Keith.

– Good game, huh? I asked.

– Yeah, Keith said.

– Looks like the Pirates might take it.

– Yeah.

We kept walking, about a half a mile an hour. Any slower and we'd be going backwards, like my dad says when we're in a traffic jam.

– Keith? I asked.

– Yeah?

– What was that stuff you said to your baba?

He said it again. It was Ukrainian, so I can't write it.

– What does it mean? I asked.

– I'm not sure, Keith said.

– You mean you just say stuff to her that you don't even know?

– No. I mean, I don't know what it means, but she does.

– Oh.

I still didn't really get it.

– Keith? I asked again.

– Yeah?

He was starting to sound annoyed.

– How do you know she understands it, if you don't even know what you're saying?

Keith stopped in the middle of the sidewalk and rolled his eyes at me.

– Because, he said. My mum taught me some words. I learned them by the sound. It's in case I need to tell Baba stuff while Mum's out at work. The stuff I just said means I'll be right back.

– So you do know what it means.

– Uh. Yeah. But only because my mum told me. I'm taking her word for it.

– Are you sure you said the right words?

– What do you mean?

– I mean, are you sure you don't get the words mixed up? That would be easy to do, since you don't even know what they mean.

Keith rolled his eyes again.

– Look, he said. You try talking in a language you don't understand. It's not easy. Besides, it doesn't even matter what I say.

– What do you mean?

– I mean, she can't hear anyway, barely. I could have been saying 'Bye, Baba, I'm running away to go on a raft down the Mississippi.' She still would have just smiled. She's practically deaf. You heard how loud she had the TV.

– I'm not so sure, I said.

– What about? Keith asked.

– I mean, I'm not so sure she doesn't understand. I got the feeling she understood me, and I didn't even say anything. I think she was kind of reading my mind, like the Amazing Kreskin.

Keith was quiet for a second, then he started giggling a bit.

– What's so funny? I asked.

– I was just picturing Baba on TV, with the Amazing Kreskin, helping him read people's minds.

I thought it was a pretty funny idea, too.

– Yeah, I said. She could sit there with her walking stick, telling which guys in the audience were thinking about naked ladies. They'd have to be Ukrainian, though.

– Who? The naked ladies?

– No, the guys who were thinking about them. If they were thinking in English, she wouldn't be able to read their minds.

– Yes, she would, numb nuts.

– How?

– Because you don't think in words. You think there's a little typewriter inside your brain or something? You think in pictures.

– Oh yeah.

We kept strolling. We were in front of the Santuccis' store. It had a sign in the window saying 'Closed for special occasion.' Something was bugging me, so I decided to ask Keith about it.

– Keith?

– Yeah?

– Are you sure your baba's okay?

– What do you mean, okay?

– I mean, are you sure it's all right for her to be alone with your dad?

He didn't say anything for a minute. When he did, I couldn't hear him.

– What? I asked.

– I said, my dad's not gonna do anything. Not now. He couldn't swat a fly now, even if he wanted to.

– Oh. Okay.

Things went quiet again for a minute, until I noticed that Keith had completely stopped walking. He seemed to be looking right at my mouth.

– What's that on your breath? he asked.

– I told you, I said. Tahiti Treat. The same stuff I spilled on my shirt.

– Oh yeah. I forgot. Tahiti Treat.

– It is, I said.

I'm a lousy liar.

– Okay, Keith said. It's Tahiti Treat. For a minute I thought it smelled like something else.

– Like what?

Stupid question.

– Just something else. Forget about it.

– Okay.

I thought about telling him the truth, but this seemed like one of those times when maybe it was better to lie, even if the other person could tell you were lying. We walked on some more, past the Gulf station towards St Mary and O'Connor. Then Keith stopped and looked at me again.

– Hey, he said.

– What? I asked.

– You're moving.

I nearly dumped myself. Here we were, walking around

talking about all kinds of stuff, and I hadn't even told Keith I was moving. *He* told *me.* Weird.

– How did you know? I asked.

– How did I know? Jeez, it was all over the place after school. Sister Arlene announced it to your class. Freddy told me about it. He told me a bunch of stuff, about how you got in trouble and took off. He kept saying 'Heavy, man, heavy' over and over again. Wow. I guess because so much stuff kept happening, even after school, I'd sort of forgotten about what happened in class, and how wild it must have looked to everyone else.

– Wow, I said.

– Yeah, Keith said. Sister took off for the office, wanting to give you the strap, but when she came back to the class, she looked all different. Mr Horvath must have talked her out of it, like that time he let me get away with farting. So Sister gave a speech about how you were leaving, and what a fine young man you were. Freddy said she didn't even notice you were gone, and the baseball cards were gone from her desk. She was probably still pretty mad. Nobody in the class had the nerve to tell her what happened. Freddy said it was the coolest thing he ever saw. Boy, you got pretty lucky.

– What do you mean?

– I mean, if you weren't leaving, you'd be in deep shit. I guess that's how you thought you'd get away with it. Wow. Way to go.

– That's not how, I said.

– What?

– I mean, I don't know how I thought I'd get away with it. When I did it, I didn't even know I was moving. I didn't really know what I was doing. I just knew I had to do it. I had to see what that last card was. You know how it is.

– Yeah.

That was true. Keith's the one guy I know who would understand something like that. And maybe Chris.

– Hold it a minute, though, Keith said. You didn't know you were moving? Not even this afternoon?

– No.

– So when did you find out?

– Right around suppertime.

– Oh.

I didn't bother explaining to Keith why I didn't know. It was pretty complicated.

– So when are you going? Keith asked.

– Tomorrow morning.

– Oh.

By this time we were past O'Connor, right across from St Paul's. It's weird to see your school all dark and empty. It's hard to believe it's the same place where you and all your friends go every day. What made it even weirder was knowing I wouldn't be going there any more. I tried not to think about it.

We cut across the O'Connor parking lot and went up by the running track. Way off, across the field, I could see a light in the Winchesters' living-room window. Without thinking about it, me and Keith started walking around the running track, with the little brown pebbles crunching under our feet. This was the same track where I used to pretend I was a marathon runner. *Wide World of Sports* had a thing once about Abebe Bikila, that Ethiopian guy who won the Olympic marathon, running twenty-six miles over cobblestones in his bare feet. One day I thought I'd try a marathon on the track barefooted, but after about half a lap my ribs were all achy, and my feet were starting to get scraped and cut up. I'd still like to do it some day, when my feet are tougher.

When we got to the curve on the track by the Beach, I thought it would be neat to go over and lie on it. Lots of times, looking out the window from St Paul's at all the high school students tanning and playing Frisbee and just hanging out, I've daydreamed about doing it myself. I figured this was a good time to try it, even though doing it with just one friend, in the dark, wasn't quite the same as being with a hundred other people on a sunny afternoon.

– Let's go lie on the Beach, I said.

– Sure, Keith said.

TWENTY-ONE

We went about halfway down the slope that ended at the
sidewalk, and lay down flat on our backs. The grass wasn't too
cold, maybe because it was too dead and brown to be very dewy.
It was actually pretty comfortable. Looking up, we could see that
it was a totally clear night, with tons of stars in the sky. Lying
there, I thought of that Beatles song, 'The Fool on the Hill', about
a guy who sits on top of a hill smiling and watching the world
turn.

    – Hey, Keith, I said.

    – Yeah?

    – You know that song by the Beatles, 'The Fool on the Hill'?

    – You mean by Sergio Mendes.

Keith's parents have this album by him, sort of like Herb
Alpert, with Mexican-style Beatles songs on it.

    – Okay, I said. He does it too. It's about this guy who watches
the world spin around after the sun goes down.

    – Well, what about it?

    – Well, can you really do that?

    – Do what?

    – Watch the world spin around? I mean, wouldn't you have to
be out in space to watch the earth spin? How could you do it
from the earth?

    – Easy, Keith said. You just pick one spot in the sky, like a
star, and keep staring at it. After a while, that star will be way
over at the other end of the sky, but it's not moving. The earth is.
You can sort of feel the earth spinning. That's what they're
talking about in that song.

    – Are you sure stars don't move? They just sit there?

    – Yeah. That's why you can always find them, if you know
where to look. I mean, you don't see one star from the Big Dipper
just go wandering off, do you? It stays there.

    – I guess.

We stared up some more. Twice Keith said, 'Look! A shooting
star!' but by the time I looked where he was pointing, they'd be

gone. I tried to find one myself, but the trouble with shooting stars is, unless you happen to be looking right at the spot where they start, you only ever see them out of the corner of your eye. They're too fast. I thought of a question.

– Hey, Keith.

– Yeah?

– If stars don't move, then why do shooting stars shoot? Why don't they just sit there?

He didn't answer at first.

– Keith? Why do shooting ...

– Look. Here's the story. They call them shooting stars, but they're not really stars. They just call them that to make it easier to say. It sounds good. They're really asteroids.

– Shooting asteroids?

– Yeah.

– Oh.

I forgot about shooting asteroids and thought about Dr Suzuki's show about the solar system that I saw on TV once, and what he said about dead stars.

– Hey, Keith, I said.

– Yeah?

– You see that star out there?

– Which one, raisin balls? There's about a billion of them.

– That one over by the Big Dipper's handle.

– What about it?

– It might not be there.

– What's that supposed to mean, it might not be there? It's right there.

– Maybe not.

– What are you talking about?

– Just because we can see it, that doesn't mean it's there.

– You mean it might be just an optical illusion?

– No. Well, sort of. What I mean is, it might be so far away that by the time we can see it, it's not there any more.

– What?

– It's true. Think about how big the universe is.

– It's pretty big.

– Yeah. Now think about the speed of light.

– How fast is that?

– I forget. Something really fast. But the universe is so big,
that by the time the light from a star gets to us, it might be, like,
ten zillion light years later, and the star might not even be there
any more. It's called a dead star.
– Wild.
– Yeah.
We lay there quiet for a minute until Keith asked something.
– Hey, Neil.
– Yeah?
– Could you do the same thing with people?
– What do you mean?
– I mean, let's say it was really dark, and a person was
standing with a flashlight way far away. Could that person be
dead?
– Not really.
– Why?
– Because the earth's not big enough. The guy with the
flashlight couldn't stand far enough away. Anybody you can see
on the earth is going to be still alive.
– But let's just say the earth was big enough, as big as the
universe. Then it could be true. You could be looking at
somebody who died a long time ago.
– I guess. Yeah, you could.
We lay there for a while more, staring up at the stars,
wondering which ones might be dead. It creeped me out a bit. I
wondered about life in the universe. What if some of those dead
stars we were seeing were really planets, with people, all Star
Trekky looking, living on them? Then I thought, that couldn't be
true. Any star you could see from that far away would be way too
hot and fiery for anybody to live on, even with special fire-
resistant suits.
I heard Keith's voice again.
– Hey, Neil.
– Yeah?
– Do you know any dead people?
– What?
– I mean, do you know anybody who's died?
– Lots of people have died.
– No. I mean, did anybody you know ever die?

- Oh, that's what you mean.
- Yeah. Well?
- Well, what?
- *Did* they?
- Not really.
- What do you mean, not really? They either died or they didn't.
- What I mean is, nobody I really know has died. I know about people who've died, like my dad's dad, but that was before I was born. Nobody I know has died since I've been alive.

That was true. Our cat Snowball died when she dug her claws too deep in a telephone line in the alley behind our house. The claws got stuck and she just hung there dead until one of the telephone guys climbed up and got her down. By that time, she was all stiff. But Snowball didn't count for the kind of stuff Keith was asking.

- So you've never had that feeling, of somebody dying? Keith asked.
- Well, once, sort of, I said.
- When was that?
- It was a little while ago, just after summer holidays started, I said.
- So? What happened?

Keith really wanted to hear the story, so I started to tell it. First I asked a question.

- You know that song 'Light My Fire', by the Doors?
- You mean by Sergio Mendes.
- No, by the bloody Doors! They did it first!
- Okay, okay, by the Doors. What about it?
- I just wanted to make sure you knew who the Doors were, for the story. Anyway, one day last summer, I was home all by myself. That hardly ever happens. I think everybody else was at Klondike Days or something. It was kind of exciting, being all alone. So I'm sitting there, on the living room floor, sorting my baseball cards. You know how you make little piles for all the different teams?
- Yeah.
- So I'm doing that, and listening to CHED. They were playing great stuff, the Guess Who, Creedence, 'Brown Sugar', 'Draggin'

the Line'. The sun was going down, so the sky outside was all pink. The living-room curtains were wide open, and the lights in the house were off, so all this weird pink light was coming into the room, filling the whole place. It felt like being in a giant fishbowl. Then this song called 'Riders on the Storm' came on.

– By the Doors?

– Yeah. Do you know it?

– No. I was just guessing.

– Yeah. So anyway, it comes on. The weird thing was, it came on when the song before wasn't even close to being over. They just faded out the other song all of a sudden, and started playing this other one by the Doors. I've never heard them do that before.

– Weird.

– Yeah. So it comes on, and it's this really spooky-sounding song. It starts off with the sound of a thunderstorm, then there's this really slow electric piano and echoey guitar music. It takes a long time for the singer to come in. The music, I don't know, sort of pulled me in. I forgot about the baseball cards, and just sat there on the rug, staring out at the sky and listening to the song. The light outside was turning from pink to red and purple, until it looked like the room was on fire.

– Wow.

– Yeah. And then, the singer's voice comes in. It was all deep and whispery. For a while, I forgot I was listening to the radio. It was like the singer was right in the room with me, whispering into my ear while this spooky music played. I've seen pictures of the singer, so I had this real clear picture of his face in my mind while all this was going on. The words to the song were really spooky too. And I don't mean goofy spooky, like watching *Frankenstein* or something. I mean, I was really scared.

I looked over at Keith. He was just staring straight up. I continued the story.

– So the words to the song were all this stuff about a hitchhiker. He's out on a highway, in the middle of nowhere, in the middle of the night, trying to hitch a ride, and there's a thunderstorm starting. A family, with kids and stuff, is driving along and they see him. The driver, probably the father, is thinking about picking this guy up. What they don't know is, the guy's a killer.

– The hitchhiker?

– Yeah. Scary. But the weird thing is, the singer sounds really scary himself. He's warning the family about this guy, but it almost sounds like he might *be* the guy. The singer might be the killer.

– Oh, jeez.

– So I'm sitting there by myself, in this fiery red room, and I can't stop listening to this song that might be being sung by a killer, and it feels like the killer is right there in the room with me. I can't see him clearly, but his face is kind of floating around.

– Wow.

– Yeah. And the song goes on and on. It was even longer than 'Hey Jude', I think. There were these long solos on electric piano and guitar, with every now and then the sound of thunder in the background. The music, like the singer, was soft, so you felt like you had to keep listening hard just to hear what was going on. That made it even creepier than if it was loud. Just when I thought I couldn't take any more, the music started to fade, like lots of songs do at the end. It took a long time to finish, but finally it did, and when it did, the radio was just silent for a minute. No other song came on, no commercial, the deejay didn't start blabbing. Nothing. Then, at last, a voice came on. It was the deejay, but he wasn't talking in his normal deejay voice. He sounded more like an ordinary person.

– What did he say?

– All he said was 'Jim Morrison. Dead at twenty-seven.'
Neither one of us said anything for a minute. Then Keith did.

– Neil?

– Yeah?

– Who's Jim Morrison?

– He was the singer. For the Doors. The guy who sang the song.

– Holy shit.

– Yeah. So I'm sitting there, still kind of in shock. It's pretty dark by now. The baseball cards are on the floor in front of me, but I can barely see them. I looked down at the cards in my hand, and they were practically ruined because I was sweating so hard. I got up and ran to the light switch and turned it on. The next song on the radio, I forget which one, was happier, but still for a while I was shaking, like I'd just seen somebody get killed or something. A bit later, everybody got home, and Mum could tell by looking at me that something must have happened, so she asked me what was wrong, but I couldn't make myself tell the story, I was too creeped by it. I just told her I was fine. The next day there was a thing in the paper about it. He died by drowning in a bathtub in France. I guess the water must have been too deep. I told my sister Susan the story, and she told me that the song I heard was the last song the Doors did. Like they *knew*.

    – Wow. Good story.

    – Thanks.

    – But, uh, I have a question.

    – Yeah? What?

    – What happened? In the song, I mean. Did they pick the guy up? Did he kill them?

    – I don't know.

    – What do you mean, you don't know?

    – I mean, they don't say, in the song, what happened next. The words, after the ones I told you, don't continue that story. They're about something else, a woman loving a man or something.

    – That's stupid.

    – Stupid?

    – Yeah. They should tell you. You can't just start a story and not finish it. That's not fair.

    – I guess not. But maybe he didn't want to finish it. Maybe he thought it would be scarier that way.

    – It's still not fair.

    – Or maybe he was going to do another song later, to continue the story. To tell everybody what happened to the family.

    – Well, he can't do that now, can he?

    – Nope.

    – So I guess we'll never know.

    – I guess not.

    – Neil?

    – Yeah?

    – Let's stop talking about this, okay?

    – Okay.

I was kind of glad to stop talking about Jim Morrison. There didn't seem to be much more to say anyway. They still play 'Riders on the Storm' on CHED sometimes, but I usually leave the room when it comes on.

TWENTY-TWO

We didn't say anything for a minute after that. It was starting to
get a bit colder. The ground wasn't so comfortable any more, so
we sat up and brushed the dead grass off ourselves. People across
the street were coming out of St Paul's church. That's where
they were voting in the election for mayor, in the church
basement. It felt funny just sitting there, so I said the first thing
that came into my head.

– The game's probably over by now, I said.

– What game? Keith asked.

– What do you mean, what game? The World Series game. It
started at six, so it's probably almost over.

– Oh yeah.

– You must have seen the first six innings or so, I said.

– Not really, Keith said.

I remembered Keith's dad on the couch, and the empty bottles.
I guess I wouldn't have wanted to watch a game in that room,
either.

– Hey, Keith, I said.

– Yeah?

– You want to hurry back to my place, and try to catch the
end? We might be able to.

– Not really, Keith said.

– Come on, I said. Let's try.

– I don't *want* to, okay? It's probably over anyway, like you
said.

– I guess.

I felt disappointed about it, but the weird thing was, the
feeling didn't last long. It just didn't seem worth it, to argue about
it. A Series game on, and I was sitting out in a field. Pretty
unusual.

– That reminds me of something, though, Keith said.

– What does?

– Talking about baseball. It reminds me. I almost forgot. I have
something to give you.

He started rooting around in his satchel. He pulled out an apple core, a yo-yo without a string, a whole bunch of stuff, before he found what he was looking for. It was a white envelope. He held it out to me.

– Freddy wanted me to give you this, he said.

– Freddy?

– Yeah. It's sort of from him and me.

– What is it?

– Just take it and find out, numb nuts, before my arm falls off.

I took it. It was so light it felt empty at first, but then I felt something small inside. I could see a bit of writing on the outside, so I turned the envelope in the direction of the streetlight to read it. In little letters it said, 'For a brother.' That was all. I could feel my heart start to pound a bit harder. The envelope wasn't licked shut, so it was easy to open. I pulled out what was inside and held it in the light. At first I couldn't believe what I saw. I thought it must have been some kind of trick. But it was real.

It was the Clemente card. Right there in my hand. 'Pirates', in big yellow letters across the top, with 'roberto clemente – outfield' (no capitals), just underneath. In the picture, which I sort of knew from the times Chris Ditka flashed his card at me, Clemente wasn't doing one of those corny poses most players do, like pretending to swing a bat or jump for a ball. He didn't have a big grin like most players do, either. Instead he was just standing there by the dugout with his hands on his hips, giving the poor photographer a look like this was the last thing on earth he wanted to do, pose for some dumb card, so hurry up. While I was looking at the picture, trying not to shake too hard, Keith started telling how he and Freddy got the card.

– It was just after school today, he said. Freddy was pretty sad about you leaving, I think. I mean, he didn't say it, but you could tell he wasn't exactly happy. He kept saying, 'Heavy, heavy, we gotta do something for the brother. Heavy.'

Wow. Freddy calling me a brother. That was a big deal. It put me right up there with Sly Stone and Muhammad Ali.

– So we're standing there by the monkey bars, Keith said. We're thinking about what to do, when we see Chris Ditka over by the crosswalk. He's standing with the grade ones and twos, waiting for the school patrols to let him across. What an idiot. Freddy says 'I've got an idea' and we start following Chris. We caught up to him by St Mary. Chris didn't even hear us coming. Freddy grabbed one of his arms, and I sort of caught on and grabbed the other one. We took him over by the side of St Mary, by the bike racks.

– What did you do to him? I asked.

The story was starting to sound a bit scarier than I thought it would.

– Well, Keith said, Chris was trying not to look scared at first. He was trying to act all tough, asking what was going on and stuff. Freddy stuck his face right up to Chris and said 'Instant karma time, Chris.'

– Wow, I said.

– Yeah, Keith said. Chris had no idea what he was talking about. Uh, do *you* know what he was talking about?

– Oh, yeah, I said. Me and Freddy talked about it today. It's this song, that says if you do bad things, bad things will happen to you.

– Oh, okay, that makes sense then, because after Freddy said that, he said to Chris, 'You have got something. Something a friend of ours wants. And we are going to take it from you.' Chris was starting to panic a bit, and I was feeling nervous, too. I mean, I've never done that kind of thing before, grabbing a guy and saying I was going to take something from him. It was exciting, but I actually still didn't know what Freddy was talking about. I didn't know what the thing was that he wanted. So finally Chris asked him what he was talking about, and I was glad, because that meant I didn't have to ask. So Freddy leaned up to Chris again and said, 'I am going to say one word, and you will know what to do. That word is Clemente.' Chris is really flooding his underwear by now. He knows we know he has the card on him, because he brings it to school every day.

– I know, I said. He only brings it to wave in my face.

I was getting mad at Chris all over again just thinking about it, so mad that I forgot for a minute that I was holding the Clemente in my hand. It was mine now. Keith kept telling what happened.

– So Chris starts saying stuff like, 'Why should I give it to you? It's mine. Finders keepers,' and Freddy goes, 'Maybe you're right. Maybe you should keep it. Maybe we should do something else instead.' Chris goes 'What's that'? and Freddy says 'Maybe you'd like to accompany us over to Santucci's store. Maybe you could explain to old man Santucci the problems he's been having with inventory in the area of baseball cards.'

    – Wow, I said.

    – Yeah, Keith said. Freddy's pretty smart. So he says to Chris, 'We are going to release your arms. I do not need to tell you what to do next.' So we let him go, and Chris pulls out this huge stack of cards from his inside jacket pocket, takes off the elastic, shuffles till he finds the Clemente, and hands it to Freddy. Freddy says, 'You have done the right thing,' and turns and starts walking away. I followed him, and then Chris started following us, saying how he would have given you the card anyway, trying to be buddies with us, talking all this weird sportscaster talk. I even felt sort of sorry for him. We just ignored him. It was great. I felt like Robin Hood.

    – Wow, I said. That's the best story I ever heard. Wow.

    – Yeah, Keith said. So we stopped off at the drug store and Freddy bought one envelope, for like two cents, wrote on it, gave it to me and told me to give it to you.

    I thought that was weird, that Freddy made Keith give it. Then I remembered another thing. Freddy was supposed to call me about maybe coming over to watch the game tonight, the same one Keith was supposed to come over for, but he never did.

    – Why did he give it to you? I asked Keith.

    – I asked him that, too, Keith said. I said, 'It was your idea, you did all the work, you should give it to him.' He just said, 'Not me, man. Goodbye speeches are not my scene. Too heavy. Too heavy.'

    I could practically see Freddy, shaking his head back and forth, making his afro go all wobbly.

    We stood up and stretched and yawned. I put the Clemente really carefully into my shirt pocket, not my pants pocket, to make sure it didn't get bent or wrinkled. A few hours before, I was thinking that baseball cards weren't so important any more, but now having that Clemente felt like the coolest thing in the world.

    – Well, I said to Keith, I guess you better go back home, eh?

– Huh?

– You better be getting back. You told your baba you were going to be right back.

– Oh. Yeah.

We started walking, back in the direction of 132nd, but after just a few steps, Keith stopped. At first I thought he might have been tying a shoelace or picking his nose or something, but when I looked back at him, he was just standing there, with his hands in his pockets, staring at the ground. I went back to wait for him. It was too dark to really see his face.

– Keith? I said. Are you okay?

He didn't answer, just kept staring down.

– Keith, I said. Come on. Let's get back.

He kept not answering, but at least he started walking again. But then he stopped like before. This time he said something.

– Neil?

– Yeah?

– It's …

– It's what? I asked.

He kept staring down straight in front of him. His chin was practically dug into his chest, so when he finally talked, his voice sounded kind of funny, like people who've had their jaws wired shut.

– It's too bad you're moving, he said.

It's really hard to explain how I felt right at that minute. There's only one thing I can think of, to compare it to. One time, in grade three, I was playing basketball on rec night at St Paul's gym. It's one of those times when anybody can do whatever they want, so you'll get some people playing basketball, some playing dodgeball, some playing tag or whatever, all at the same time. It gets pretty nuts. So anyway, I went up to grab a rebound, and right then, when I was in mid-air, these two little kids who were running around with the tug-of-war rope came up behind me. They weren't watching where they were going. Just as I was doing my Wilt Chamberlain thing, slamming the ball into my free hand, I felt the rope behind my ankles. It flipped me back until I was staring straight up at the gym lights, and then I fell flat on my back on the floor. All the air went shooting out of me. I wasn't unconscious, but I couldn't breathe and I couldn't call for help. People were standing around looking down at me, some of them giggling because my mouth was moving but no words were coming out. It's called having the wind knocked out of you. So that's kind of how it was, standing there in the field with Keith. I wanted to say something, but I just couldn't make myself. When your best friend tells you he's sorry you're moving, it's different from finding out about it from your mum. You know you're going to keep seeing your mum, even if it's in a different place, but it's not the same with your friends. I think it wasn't until Keith said that that I really, totally, knew I was moving. All kinds of questions were going through my head. How was I supposed to finish reading *The Horse Who Played Center Field*? What about my Clemente art project? How was I going to see how Daniela's Brazil picture turned out, or see if Leslie Gibson and Carl Wysocki started talking more in class? What about the toothpick races, and hanging out with Freddy talking about soul music, or going to Northgate for CHED charts and jujubes? No matter what I thought about, it was something I wouldn't be doing any more. It was like what Keith said about the Doors song, how it wasn't fair not to know how it ended.

It was right then, wishing I knew how things were going to end, that I got an idea. Thinking about it now, I can see that it probably wasn't the brightest idea ever. If I could do it again, I'd probably just keep my mouth shut, but at that minute it seemed to make sense, so I told Keith about it.

– Hey, Keith, I said.

– What?

– You don't like where you're living now, right?

– What are you talking about? he asked.

He was still staring down, talking in the locked-jaw voice.

– I mean, things aren't very good at your place now, right? I asked.

– It's not exactly home sweet home, if that's what you mean, Keith said. It's not *Leave It to Beaver*.

– Well, I said, I've got an idea.

– Oh yeah? What's that?

– I mean, I don't want to move, and you're not happy at home, right?

– What about it?

– Remember when you told me about where your baba used to live?

– What, you mean on the acreage?

– No. I mean when she came to Canada. At first. You told me she lived in a hole in the ground.

– Yeah. She did.

– You told me it was actually pretty comfortable, for a hole.

– That's what they say.

– Well, what about it, then? I asked.

– What about what?

– What about you and me, going to live in a hole in the ground?

– What?

– Yeah. We could go out to one of those acreages. I bet some of those old holes are still there. We could find branches and leaves and stuff for a roof, and find some old furniture. It wouldn't be that bad. We could go to the bathroom out in the woods, in a smaller hole.

– I don't know.

– You don't know what? Why couldn't we? For food we could have a little garden. In the winter, we wouldn't even need a fridge. *Outside* would be our fridge. We could trap rabbits and stuff. We could live close enough to a town so we could still go in to buy chocolate bars and baseball cards and stuff.

– Uh, what would we buy them with?

– What do you mean?

– I mean, genius, what about money?

– We could help out farmers with their harvest and stuff. They'd pay us.

– The farmers would pay us?

– Yeah.

– They'd say, 'Here's your cash, boys. Now off you go, back to your hole.'

– Yeah! And after a while, we'd have enough money to build a dirt house, and after that a real house.

– A homestead.

– Yeah! You've got it!

– Two little boys, in their home on the range.

– Yeah!

– Neil?

– Yeah?

– Can I tell you something?

– Yeah.

– That's the stupidest, most idiotic, retarded thing I've ever heard in my life.

– What is? The part about building a house? I didn't mean *we'd* build it. We'd pay other guys.

– No.

– No what?

– No, I didn't mean the part about building the house. I mean the whole thing. The whole idea is completely retarded.

– But listen, we could ...

– No.

Keith's voice was getting louder. He wasn't staring at the ground any more.

– Listen to me, he said. You just don't get it, do you?

– Get what?

Keith took a deep breath.

– Let me ask you something, he said.

– Sure, I said.

– Why do you think my baba lived in a hole in the ground?

– You told me. Because they didn't have time to build a house before the winter came.

– No. I'm not talking about the weather. Why do you think they were there in the first place? Why do you think they had to leave their home?

I have to admit, I'd never really thought about it. I guessed.

– Well, probably for the same reasons most people move, I said.

– Oh, yeah? What reasons are those?

– Well, stuff like needing a bigger place, or the dad getting a better job someplace else.

– A better job and a bigger place.

– Yeah.

– Wrong.

– What?

– I said, you're wrong. Oh, man. Do you really think ...

I was beginning to realize I'd been saying some things that

were maybe a bit stupid. Keith was getting so mad it was hard for him to talk. He dug his hands so hard into his pockets I thought they'd break through, and ground his feet into the dead grass.

– Uh, Keith? I asked.

– What?

– Why did they move, then?

He took another deep breath.

– Okay, he said. Here's the story. They didn't *move*. Not like you're moving. It wasn't their idea, okay? They *left*. And the reason they left is because if they didn't, they would have died.

– Died?

– Yeah. Died. Starved to death, or got shot.

– Why?

– Why? Because there were people there who didn't think people should have their own little farms. They thought everything should be one big farm. And if you didn't like that, if you didn't want to work on a giant farm, you had three choices. You could starve to death. You could get shot. Or you could take off. Dad told me all this. My mum doesn't know he's telling me. I don't think she wants me to know this stuff. But sometimes, when Mum's not home and Dad's been drinking, he tells me stuff.

– Oh.

I couldn't think of anything to say.

– And another thing, Keith said. What makes you think you're the same as me?

– What do you mean?

– I mean, you talk about us running away together. You talk like your problems are just as bad as my problems.

– I didn't mean that. I just meant …

– But you *said*. You said you didn't want to move, and I wasn't happy at home, so we should run away and live in a hole. Like our problems were the same.

– Yeah, but …

– Yeah, *but*, our problems are *not* the same. You're going to go with your happy family, with your dad who goes hunting and takes you golfing, from one nice house to another nice house somewhere else. What's so bad about that? It sounds like a pretty good deal to me.

– But I don't want to move. I want to stay …

– You still don't get it, do you? You don't get how it's different to come home from school, and your mum's not home because she has to work two jobs because your dad can't work, and your dad can't work because he's passed out half the time, and when he's not passed out he's trying to *get* passed out, and your grandmother is there because she's supposed to be taking care of you but there's nothing she can really do, because she can hardly move, and you can't speak her language and she can't speak yours. That's pretty different from just not feeling like moving.

– I guess, I said.

– Yeah, Keith said. You guess. Well, guess *this*!

He gave me the finger.

I couldn't believe it. I stood there, not knowing what to do or say, and before I knew it, Keith was taking off in the direction of his place, with his satchel bouncing on his back. By the time I knew what was happening, it was way too late to try to catch up with him. He was too far away.

I don't know how you're supposed to know what to do when something like that happens. It's not fair. Nobody ever teaches you. In school, you learn how to spell, and write paragraphs, and draw, and play dodgeball, but nobody ever says, 'This is what you do when your best friend gives you the finger because you said something idiotic, and he takes off, and you're moving the next day.' I guess what I should have done was try to chase after Keith, and tell him I was sorry, but the trouble was I was too shocked to run, and even if I caught up with him, I wasn't sure what I was supposed to be sorry for. Okay, so the living in a hole idea was pretty stupid, but the reason I said it was good. All I really wanted to say was we both weren't happy, so it would be neat to go someplace where we could be happy. Keith got mad because he thought his reasons for not being happy were better than mine. He was probably right. Okay, he *was* right. But I still didn't mean to make him mad. I meant to do the opposite. I hate that, when you try to do one thing and something else happens, especially when the thing you were trying to do was good, or at least you thought it was good. It's not fair.

TWENTY-THREE

I really should have gone home right then. It was already later than I'd ever been out by myself before. There was even still a chance of seeing the end of the baseball game. But something stopped me. Maybe it was because I would have had to go right past Keith's place, and I was still too chicken. I couldn't get the picture out of my head, of Keith's middle finger, and his satchel bouncing around as he ran away. It seemed like I should be able to stop everything and back it up, like in the hockey highlights. I'd make Keith run back, and I wouldn't say the stuff I said. But you can't do that. Stuff happens once, and that's it.

So instead of going home, I turned around and walked the other way, toward 82nd Street. I wasn't really thinking about where I was going, I just went, through a crowd of people talking about the election, past the church and the row housing where Tommy Winchester lives. That's when I saw Irene's Café, and did the stuff I told about at the start of the book.

Way back then, I said Mr Baldwin told me I should write about everything that happens in a day, and I said I would, but I skipped what happened between leaving Irene's and starting to write, so I'll tell it now.

On the way home from Irene's, I was still pretty upset about some of the stuff that happened that day, mostly finding out I was moving and getting given the finger by Keith. Some stuff, like scoring the touchdown and getting thrown around by those Italian girls, was actually pretty cool, but mostly it was the kind of day that upsets you. The funny thing was, though, that I was cheered up a bit from talking to Mr Baldwin at Irene's, and thinking how he thought I was smart enough to write a book. Getting the Clemente was great, too. I kept feeling it there in my pocket all the way home.

When I finally got back to the house, the clock was off the kitchen wall, so I had to dial 421-1111 to find out what time it was. I couldn't believe it when the robot lady said nine o'clock.

That meant I'd only been out for two and a half hours. It felt more like a year.

The house was pretty much empty, but I could hear the TV, which was normally in the basement, coming from the living room. I went in there, thinking maybe I'd check on the game, and Susan was there, lying on her stomach on the floor, watching a movie. The movie was about this guy, driving a car across a desert in the States, who starts getting followed by this giant truck. The guy in the car doesn't know why the truck is after him. They never show the truck driver. The only talking in the movie is by the guy in the car, talking to himself about how weird it is that this truck is chasing him. It was pretty exciting. I sat down and watched it with Susan for a while, until I thought of a question.

– Hey, Susan.

– What?

She kept looking at the screen. I didn't blame her. The truck was trying to ram the car from behind.

– Where is everybody?, I asked.

It was a natural question. Nobody else was around.

Susan didn't answer right away. The car was swerving off the road, crashing into all these cages full of rattlesnakes and tarantulas and stuff. This little old lady, who owned the reptile zoo, was pretty mad about all the damage. The car just kept going, while the snakes and spiders slithered and crawled around free.

– Dad's out voting, Susan said. Everybody else is at the A&W. They met there for burgers and root beer.

– Uh, Susan?

– What?

– Were Mum and Dad mad?

– Mad about what?

– About me not being there.

– Oh. No. Dad said you were probably watching the hockey game at your friend's house.

– Baseball.

– What?

– It was a baseball game. The World Series.

– Oh.

Susan's not exactly a sports buff.

We kept watching the movie. The driver of the car was so freaked out by this giant truck on his tail that he was chewing on his lip, and pretty soon blood started dribbling down his chin.

Then our phone rang. With the house so empty, it was as loud as an explosion. Susan jumped up and ran to it in about half a second. She must have thought it was one of her boyfriends. I watched the movie by myself for a few seconds. The car and truck were headed straight for a cliff. I heard Susan's voice.

– Neil?

I had to force myself to look away from the screen.

– Yeah?

– The phone.

– What about it?

– It's for you.

It never even occurred to me, that it might be for me. I never get phone calls. If I want to talk to one of my friends, or they want to talk to me, we just go over. Plus it was so late.

– Who is it? I asked.

– I don't know, Susan said. *She* didn't say.

Susan raised one eyebrow when she said 'she'. She was trying to bug me.

That was even weirder than getting a phone call, to be getting one from a she. Walking to the phone, I tried to think of who it might be. I hoped maybe it was one of those Italian girls from the party, but then I realized that was pretty stupid. Teenage girls don't phone nine-year-old boys. Then I thought, oh God, what if it's Sister Arlene? She was the only other female person I could think of, right at that minute. I don't usually think of her as a lady, but she is. I said a little prayer that it wouldn't be her. I picked up the phone.

– Hello?

– Hello? Is this Neil?

It took a second to figure out the voice. Then it hit me. It was Daniela da Silva. My legs went wobbly.

– Yeah, I said. It's him. I mean, it's me.

I tried to picture Daniela at home, on the phone. I wasn't sure where she lived, but I imagined her in one of those rich people's houses on the south side, by the Valley Zoo. She probably didn't really live there, because that would be too far from school, but it was easier than trying to picture her in a row house or something.

– I thought I'd call you, she said. Given everything that's happened.

– What happened? I asked.

I thought maybe she was still mad at me for the dodgeball thing in gym, or for making fun of her for not knowing what a neurologist is. I mean, I don't know what one is either, but I don't go around saying I'm going to be one.

Daniela did one of her sighs. I could practically see her, rolling her eyes.

– Um, in case you've forgotten, you're moving, she said. Today was your last day at St Paul's.

– Oh yeah, that, I said.

I must have sounded like a dork.

– Yeah, *that*, Daniela said. Although, I must say, it's probably just as well you're moving.

– What do you mean? I asked.

– Because, if you weren't, you'd probably have been expelled, she said.

– Yeah. Probably.

– That was quite a performance you put on today.

– Yeah. I guess it was.

– Whatever possessed you, anyway? Do you have a death wish or something?

– No. I don't want to die. I just had to see that last card.

– Oh, yes. The cards. Well worth ruining your future for.

I didn't know what to say to that. I mean, what I did to get those cards was weird enough to me. To somebody like Daniela, it must have looked like, well, like I really did want to die. I thought of that Walt Disney show with all the lemmings running off a cliff, flip-flopping in slow motion and landing in the sea, and they can't even swim. Then I remembered something.

– Hey, Daniela, I said.

– Yes?

– Thanks for trying to warn me.

I was talking about when she elbowed me just before Sister Arlene caught me with the cards. I'd almost forgotten about that.

– Oh, yes. That. I must say, I don't know what came over me.

– What do you mean?

– I mean, I can't think what possessed me to put my own future career at risk to help you. If you want to disgrace yourself for the sake of some football cards, that's your affair, but why should I be dragged down with you?

– Baseball.

– Pardon me?

– They were baseball cards.

– Oh. Well, in that case it's all understandable.

Daniela was trying to sound as snotty as she usually was, but the weird thing was, it wasn't bugging me so much. I noticed that my legs weren't wobbling any more. It was almost like having just a normal conversation with somebody.

– Hey, Daniela, I said.

– Yes?

– So why did you help me?

– I told you. I don't know. Temporary insanity, maybe.

By this time, she was the one who sounded kind of nervous.

– Daniela?

– Yes?

– Why did you phone me, then?

– Pardon me?

– I mean, if you think you were crazy trying to help me, then why did you phone me?

She didn't say anything for a minute. I could hear the sound o a gigantic crash coming from the TV in the living room.

– Daniela? I asked. Are you still there?

– Yes. I'm still here.

– So why ...

– I heard your question.

She went quiet again, but this time I knew she'd answer. I let her take her time. When she did say something, it was in her ordinary person voice, the same one she used when she was talking about visiting her maid at Easter in Brazil.

– I called, she said, because I wanted to say goodbye. It was nice to have someone with at least some intellectual capacity ir the class. School will be a lot less interesting now.

My legs were shaking again, I noticed.

– It's only Londonderry, I said.

– Pardon me?

– That's where I'm moving to. It's only about thirty blocks away.

– Oh.

– You can still show me your picture.

– What?

– Your picture of Bahia. That you're doing in art class. You can still show me, when you're finished. You can look up my new number, or I can phone you, when it's finished. I can come over and look at it. It's not that far.

She didn't answer at first. I could swear I heard her, not crying, but doing that funny kind of breathing people do just before they cry. I was even starting to do it myself. Hearing other people cry always makes me want to cry. She talked again, in a shaky voice.

– Neil?

– Yeah?

– I have to go now.

– Oh.

– So, um, goodbye, then.

– Yeah, goodbye.

She hung up first. I stood there for a while, with the buzzing phone still up next to my face, like I was still going to say something. Then for one weird minute, I thought the phone was leaking or something. There was this water on the receiver, getting on my hands, making the phone slippery to hold. Then I realized the phone wasn't leaking. I was. I must have been crying. I put the receiver down and wiped my face with my shirt sleeve.

When I went to go back to the living room, Susan was standing there. I thought for sure she was going to make fun of me for talking to a girl. I braced myself for it. But she didn't. Instead, she handed me something.

– I thought you might want this, she said.

I looked down. It was the new CHED chart. It was the first time I even thought about it since breakfast.

– Thanks, I said.

– So? Susan said.

– So what? I asked.

– So what's number one?

I unfolded the chart and checked. It wasn't 'Maggie May' any more. It wasn't 'Do You Know What I Mean?', like I predicted, either. It was a new song.

– 'Gypsies, Tramps and Thieves', I said. By Cher.

– I guess she broke up with Sonny, Susan said.

– Yeah.

– What's the new album ad?

I looked. It was for one by Canned Heat. Two big fat guys with beards are in that band. One of them died a while ago. I showed Susan. She looked at it, and started singing, not any words, but imitating the sound of a guitar. Pretty soon I recognized the song. It was by Canned Heat. Since Susan was doing the music, I figured I'd sing.

– I'm on the road again, I'm on the road again, I sang.

I was trying to sound like the record, where the singer has this weird sort of robot voice.

– I'm on the road again, Susan sang back in the same kind of voice.

Neither one of us knew any of the other words, so we just sang those ones over and over. We really got into it. I didn't think of it then, but it was really the perfect song to be singing, on our last night in Glengarry. We danced around the living room like the hippies in Woodstock, singing in our robot voices.

– I'm on the road again, I'm on the road again …

* ♦ ♦

That's pretty much all that happened. Everybody got home a little bit later, we stuffed the last few things in the U-Haul, slept one last night in the house, packed our mattresses in the morning, and drove to Londonderry. I had to go back to St Paul's in the afternoon with my mum to get all my books and stuff. They were in a bag in the secretary's room. Classes were going on, so I didn't see anybody in the halls, but I did see Tommy Winchester outside, behind one of the grade two portables, reading *Man, Myth and Magic*. He didn't see me.

Before the book is over, I have to admit something. Lots of times, telling this story, I've used words like 'this morning' and 'today'. I was trying to make it look like I was saying everything the same night, in the living room in Glengarry. That's not true, though. It takes a lot longer than one night to write a book like this. Try it sometime. It was actually more like two months ago that we moved.

It's winter now, almost time for Christmas holidays. Sam keeps trying to run away, I think back to our old place. Ivor Dent won the election, so Edmonton might get an NHL team. The Pirates won the Series, in seven games. I watched the last game in our new garage, with Dad, while he plucked ducks and pulled their guts out. I was getting all excited about the game, and at the same time trying not to puke from seeing duck guts all over the place.

When the game was over and they showed the Pirates celebrating in their dressing room, Clemente did something really neat. The announcer asked him some question like 'How does it feel, Roberto?' but Clemente just ignored him and started saying something in Spanish, for his fans back home in Puerto Rico. He went on for a while. You could tell the announcer was getting kind of uncomfortable standing there holding the microphone and not understanding anything, but there was nothing he could do. He just had to nod like he knew what was going on. It was great. I've got the Clemente card in a box under my bed. I pull it out now and then and look at it. Sometimes, when Duncan and Richard aren't around, I pretend to talk to Clemente. I ask him for advice about stuff. I don't do the thing with the mountain climber on the bottom of the mattress any more.

My new school, Father Leo Green, is pretty weird. It's one of those 'open area' schools. That means it doesn't have different classrooms, just big rooms with bunches of classes together. Some classes are in the gym, because they haven't finished building the school yet. Another thing that's different is that the school doesn't have any windows, just little sort of slits here and there. You can't even see out. It's a lot harder to concentrate on your schoolwork when you can't even see what's going on outside. Also, the whole school stinks from this glue they used to stick the carpets down, and you can't let any fresh air in. It's retarded.

I haven't tried that hard yet to make new friends and stuff. I barely even know anybody's name yet, except for this one kid called Elvis Lenarduzzi. It's hard to forget that one. I think my head's still in Glengarry. Maybe now that I'm finishing the book, I'll talk to more people, and pay more attention in class.

But there's another thing, besides the book, that keeps reminding me of my old neighbourhood. I *see* it all the time. Glengarry was flat, so you couldn't really see anything else from it. It was easy to forget that there was a whole big city out there. But Londonderry is hilly, and my school is up pretty high. Right next to it, there's this even higher reservoir, where people go crazy-carpeting and tobogganing. One kid had to go to the hospital last week. He couldn't stop his crazy carpet in time, and crashed head first into the side of the school. You can still see the mark where he hit. Anyway, from the top of this hill, you can look down on the whole city. You can see the old water tower, and the CN building, and the MacDonald Hotel. And, if you know where to look, you can see Glengarry, at least the tallest things in it, like the St Paul's church steeple, and the air raid siren tower, and the giant Christmas tree on top of the Northgate liquor store.

Sometimes I'll just stand there on top of that hill, while everybody else tears past me with their crazy carpets and toboggans and pieces of cardboard. I'll try to imagine what's

184

happening there, thirty blocks away. What are Keith and Freddy and Daniela and all those people doing? It's hard to picture. In my head they're still doing exactly what they were doing when I left. I'll stand there for I don't know how long, until my feet start to freeze and I have to go home. Next spring, when I have my new bike, I'll be able to go back to Glengarry myself. I'll be able to see what's going on.

♦

ACKNOWLEDGEMENTS

In the 'this book would not have been possible' category are: Joe and Maureen McGillis for a lifetime of unstinting love and support, and for trusting – with no visible proof – that I knew what I was doing; and Padma, who, in the nicest of ways, kicked my ass until I did it. Profuse thanks go to Terry Rigelhof for believing; John Metcalf for making a hard job easy; Doris Cowan for meticulousness and sensitivity; Tim and Elke Inkster for dedication and patience; Terry Byrnes and David LeBlanc for valued artistic input. All of the following also helped, whether they know it or not: Lou Zoldan (the Oilers are mighty and shall sip from the Cup again), Melinda Mills, Maria Dunn, Andy Kurkowski, Phil and Kathy at Sorrento Centre, the Sugar Bowl Café (try their cinnamon buns), Adrian and Luci King-Edwards, The Word Bookstore and all who shop there, Ven Begamudré, Bryan Demchinsky, Catherine Bush, Eliza Clark, all of my family, Bhuvana, Vis, and Uma Viswanathan, Mark Lorenzen, Diane Nalini. To all I've left out: I'll buy you a beer. Special thanks for inspiration to Mr Bouska, Mavis Gallant and R.K. Narayan.

T.P. BYRNES

Ian McGillis was born in Hull, Quebec, grew up in Edmonton, and now lives in Montreal, within hailing distance of Fairmount Bagels. He is a regular contributor to *The Gazette* and co-edits the *Montreal Review of Books*. His journalism has also appeared in the *Globe and Mail* and the *National Post*. This is his first novel.